IN
HEMINGWAY'S
MEADOW

Award-Winning Fly-Fishing Stories

Edited by Joe Healy

FlyRod&Reel books

IN
HEMINGWAY'S
MEADOW

ISBN 978-0-89272-805-3

Library of Congress Control Number: 2009934956

Book design by Chad Hughes

Printed in the United States
5 4 3 2 1

FlyRod&Reelbooks

wwwflyrodreel.com
Distributed to the trade by National Book Network

foreword

E very now and then, you get to meet someone who has influenced
the fly-fishing world in a creative, life-sustaining way. Fortunately
for all of us, Nick Lyons and the staff of *Fly Rod & Reel* magazine—friends of John D. Voelker—collaborated with John Frey and
the Voelker Foundation to create the Robert Traver Fly-Fishing Writing Award in 1994. Nick and those friends are literary entrepreneurs,
founders whose creative powers deserve our praise. We are blessed to
have known them, to have benefited from their keen sense of truth (even
in fiction) and their knowledge and respect for the natural world where
trout are found. It is to them, and to our old pal John Voelker (known
on book covers as Robert Traver), that we dedicate this volume of Traver
Award stories, *In Hemingway's Meadow*.

We trust you will find that these stories stimulate your imagination
and recall the fun on and near the water with friends (past, present and
future), knowing that days on a trout stream are, in fact, additive to
your life total.

Robert Traver—John's chosen pen name that combined his brother's
and mother's names—was used for John's first three novels, *Trouble-
shooter*, *Danny & The Boys* and *Small Town D.A.*, published from
1943 to 1954, while he was Marquette County (Michigan) prosecutor.
"I didn't want the voters to think I was an author on company time,"

he explained. John wrote all of his books in laborious longhand, most of them on yellow legal pads with green felt pen. One afternoon at his camp on Frenchman's Pond, after teaching me his "patented roll cast" and giving me a "15-2s" lesson (as he was the Upper Peninsula cribbage champ), John asserted, "I do most of my writing during the winter months when thick ice covers my favorite fishing spots. There isn't any good writing; only re-writing. Observe, observe, observe. Then, polish your work."

His *Anatomy of a Fisherman* and *Trout Madness* have been described as the best fishing books since Izaak Walton's seventeenth century *The Compleat Angler*. Voelker's numerous articles on the joys of fly-fishing attest to his great love of the outdoors and established him as the dean of American fly-fishing. David Richcy of the *Detroit News* wrote, "Voelker could put into words the inner thoughts that few trout fishermen can express. He could draw word pictures of rising trout, the slash of a brookie to a fly, and the mystery of what trout fishing is all about."

In April 1989, John Voelker helped establish the John D. Voelker Foundation. In our first 20 years, we have invited our members to initially fund the Traver Fly-Fishing Writing Award, provide Native American law-school scholarships, commissioned Rod Crossman (a Traver Award illustrator) to paint John's Michigan Supreme Court portrait and collaborated with Trout Unlimited, FFA and Rusty Gates' Anglers of the Au Sable to restore and protect trout habitat.

Charles Kuralt, who had featured John in his CBS *On the Road* series, called John Voelker "about the nearest thing to a great man I've ever known." The 1996 Traver Awards were dedicated to Kuralt, who wrote a strong letter of support for the Traver Award Endowment Fund.

It is a privilege to have had Charles, Nick Lyons and John Frey serve on the foundation's board of directors. Nick is a renowned author and editor, whose many splendid books inspire and engender love and mysteries of trout fishing. Fortunately for Traver lovers, Nick also selected and edited Traver books, essays and letters, including manuscripts from the Voelker Papers at Northern Michigan University. The result is *Traver on Fishing*, which I encourage you to read.

Nick writes, "I'm delighted the Traver Award will continue. When we got it started we wanted to encourage stories and then essays that reflected John's ample spirit and good values in writing about fly-fishing and the natural world. The very fact that there's now an anthology coming out, gleaned from literally thousands of submissions, suggests that the program has already been a success. A number of the winners have had books published . . . and a whole lot of folk have been encouraged to write wisely and well about a subject so dear to John's heart."

What is it that so attracted people from all walks of life to this back-woods philosopher and naturalist? Voelker's famous essay "Testament of a Fisherman" provides some strong clues: "I fish because I love to; because I love the environs where trout are found, which are invariably beautiful; . . . because trout do not lie or cheat and cannot be bought or bribed, but respond only to quietude and humility and endless patience; because I suspect men are going along this way for the last time, and I for one don't want to waste the trip; . . . because only in the woods can I find solitude without loneliness; because bourbon out of an old tin cup always tastes better out there; . . . and . . . not because I regard fishing as being so terribly important but because I suspect that so many of the other concerns of men are equally unimportant—and not nearly so much fun."

It is fun to go back and re-read the Traver Award Winners and (as the award guidelines state) the other "Distinguished original stories or essays that embody the implicit love of fly-fishing, respect for the sport and the natural world in which it takes place. The Traver Stories and Essays demonstrate high literary values in three categories:

A. The Joy of Fly-Fishing: Personal or Philosophic
B. Ecological: Knowledge and Protection of the Natural World
C. Humor: Piscatorial Friendships and Fun on the Water."

Pete Fromm's "Home Before Dark" set the pace in 1994, drawing upon a fly-fishing trip between a father and stepson, providing the reader with insights and questions. As the annual 150 to 200 entries rolled in, the judges (Nick Lyons, John Frey, Charles Kuralt in 1996, the Traver Award winners, Ted Leeson, Seth Norman, the *FR&R* editors, Fred Baker, Jim Graves and I) have indeed had fun, and were challenged to select the winning stories.

Clearly, the lesson from Seth Norman's "Edith's Rule" comes to mind—connecting people is vital, but you cannot actually give it away, especially where servant leadership is concerned. In my life, it was my father who helped me see how this works. Dick Vander Veen asked a question the Traver Award asks, "Can one cultivate the ability to be creative? Marion"—(his wife, my mom)—"taught me a little of what it is to see through the eyes of an artist. She opened my mind to see that to be creative is the noblest of all activity. The grand object of life is to create something for the good of all that never existed before."

Bouncing out to Frenchman's Pond with John at the wheel of his fish car, taking time to pick blueberries and *Boletus edulus* in season and trading barbs and yarns, we talked about writing and the need to encourage young writers to polish their craft. We exchanged ideas through more than 100 letters. In his last letter, dated March 18, 1991, John kindly acknowledged a story I'd written. It was returning from Ishpeming's post office that afternoon that John's fish car—and he—ended their many U. P. adventures.

We thank those who founded and helped fund the Traver Award, 1994 to today. Now, we have work to do. For we challenge you, our readers, to join us in contributing to the Traver Award Endowment Fund so that the award is, in fact, perpetual. Please explore the Voelker Foundation Web site (www.voelkerfdn.org) and help us endow the Traver Award, and thereby protect the creative environs where trout are found, for future generations.

Richard F. (Rich) Vander Veen, III
President, John D. Voelker Foundation
July 2009

introduction

Joe Healy

When John Voelker died in March 1991, at the age of 87, we lost one of fly-fishing's finest writers. Few have equaled his ability to convey the charm and magic of fly-fishing; his writing is fun and funny; it's honest, even when it's fiction. Voelker, using his pen name Robert Traver, helped us live the sport in printed form.

This was the spirit in which *Fly Rod & Reel* helped to launch the Robert Traver Fly-Fishing Fiction Award in 1994, and to sustain it since. Sincere thanks go to the John D. Voelker Foundation, based in Lansing, Michigan, for sponsoring the award and its generous cash prize each year.

The stories selected here, all fiction with one exception, are Traver Award winners or finalists, tracing from 1994, to 2007, the year this book's eponymous piece "In Hemingway's Meadow" (the standalone essay in this collection) won. We close this book with a special story: "Frenchman's Revisited" by Robert Traver, published in *Rod & Reel* (as *Fly Rod & Reel* was then called) in 1988.

That Irish master of the short story, Frank O'Conner, instructed that short fiction should embody "an ideal action worked out in terms of verisimilitude." With that in mind, I know you'll find each of the works in this book enchanting and engaging for the truth about fly-fishing, and about life, they represent.

home before dark

Pete Fromm

M y stepson, Gordon, was already in the café when I got there, and he poured coffee for me as I sat down. He added my cream and sugar without asking, though sugar was something I'd given up a long time ago. I stared at him while he stirred the cup. We'd had dinner together the night before, with our wives, but I'd spent the night watching Sandy, my wife, his mom, worried about how she was holding up.

We ordered a quick breakfast and, because I couldn't think of anything to say, I asked, "When's the last time you went fishing?"

"Years ago. Monique isn't much of an outdoorsman. I wish she would have come though. She was pretty nervous last night, but you'd like her if you got to know her."

"I'm sure of that," I said conversationally, but Gordon gave me a quick glance, a questioning look I remembered. "If you picked her to stick with she must be a good one," I said, and it sounded as false as it was.

Gordon said, "You're the one who picked well."

"I tried to get your mom to come along," I told him. "But she thought it would be nice if just the two of us went."

"Old time's sake."

I nodded, though Sandy had stayed home thinking I might get some answers out of him alone. We looked away from each other as the waitress set the food down. After she left, I took a deep breath but wound up only asking something harmless, like "What have you been doing?" or "Where'd you and Monique meet?"

And Gordon responded with the same light chatter. We argued over the bill when it came, and I didn't mention his mother again until we were taking the canoe off the car, when I explained that Sandy and I had run the shuttle the night before. After we settled the canoe into the river Gordon stood beside it, staring out over the flow of dark water. The autumn dawn was late, and it was just growing light. Scattered flocks of geese struggled by overhead, barely visible, honking mournfully. The air was much colder than it had been the day before, wafer-thin ice rimming the stones against the bank.

"Thanks for showing this to me again," Gordon said, shivering, huddling deeper into his coat. If it'd been years and years ago, I would've run my hands up and down his sides, quick and hard, chasing away goose bumps. But I just stood quietly on the bank and watched him shiver.

"Ready?" I asked.

"And waiting," he answered, his old line.

I paddled from the stern, and Gordon was quick to strip out line and begin casting. But he was wearing big, goofy mittens, city things, and it was nearly impossible for him to hold his line. He laughed about it, and I asked if he wanted my fingerless gloves.

He shook his head without turning around and said, "I've just got to toughen up is all. I've forgotten about so much." He took off his mittens then and started casting for real. I'd forgotten how graceful he was, and I stopped paddling to watch him quarter the nymph upstream and work it across the current.

"You haven't forgotten a thing," I said.

"That's not what I expected to hear from you," he responded. He did turn then, his old challenging smile bold across his face.

"Forgotten a thing about fishing."

He waited for me to go on, his smile starting to quaver the way it did when he was in trouble as a kid, trying so hard to show he didn't care. I watched him turn away, picking up his rod, and I told myself again that I was glad to see him, glad to see him hug his mother again. But I also knew I'd never be able to forget how he'd just disappeared, how he'd left her wondering for six years. During those years I'd never doubted that we'd see him again, and I kept reassuring Sandy, whispering things about adolescent rage, the difficulties of leaving the nest, the whole time picturing that smug smile of his, wondering if I'd be able to keep from punching it from his face when he reappeared.

He had a strike then, and I've rarely been so happy to see one. His face lit up, and he lifted the rod tip just quickly enough to set the hook without pulling it away. The trout was a native, a cutthroat, not too big, and it gave up quickly. Gordon dipped his hand into the icy water, freeing the hook, releasing the fish just as I said, "Awful nice pan-size."

He looked down into the water. "I never liked killing them," he said.

"What are you talking about? We ate rivers of trout. Your mom loves them."

"That was before I knew there were so many ends to things."

Gordon looked at me, and I was shocked by the startling familiarity of his face. I remembered the odd gold bursts flecking his brown eyes. When he was a boy they'd bothered me. They were a flaw, I thought, somehow eerie. They were too light, like sheep's eyes.

Suddenly he squinted, and I knew he was smiling his real smile. "I got the first. The biggest. The smallest. The most. I'm killing you in every category."

I'd forgotten the old contest we'd developed in the years I'd tried to gentle into his father's place. "Give me time," I said, and Gordon stripped in his slack and cast again.

We both fished as much as we could, but nothing else struck before the river curved and I had to put down my rod for my paddle. Gordon retrieved his nymph, too, but instead of picking up a paddle to help, he stuck his hands under his arms.

"Whenever I thought about all this it was always the fish I remembered, and the way the river looked when the mist was just clearing. Or the way you'd get so tense going through white water, how it wasn't safe to say anything then, but afterward whatever I said was the funniest thing in the world. It was never the damn cold I remembered."

I glanced at the bottom of the canoe, the same one we'd used then. After he'd left I'd been able to forget he'd ever been with me, that he'd ever seen that kind of thing with me.

"It's never the damn cold I remember," Gordon said again, arms still wrapped tight around himself. "Or lugging all our stuff over those endless portages. Or sitting under the canoe during the downpours—black-fly bait."

"No one remembers the bad stuff," I said, realizing even as I spoke that that's exactly what I'd forced myself to remember about Gordon. "Why would anyone bother remembering that?"

"I think if you don't you'll wind up crazy," he answered, taking his hands out from under his arms and blowing on his fingers. "I can't even feel my fingers," he said. "You'd think I'd remember anything that hurt this much."

"It's your mind's trick. Blocking out the bad."

"It's a dirty trick," Gordon said, picking up his rod, his mom's rod, which I'd brought for him to use. He turned away from me, casting again. "If all you remember is the good, you wind up homesick for things that weren't really that great to begin with."

We were on another flat, quiet stretch, and I picked up my rod to change flies. The knot I tied took concentration. "It really was pretty great," I said quietly, beginning to understand how he'd worked things around after he left, worked them around so he could stand himself.

Gordon shrugged, facing away from me, and then nodded quickly. I could picture how he'd bite his lower lip, exactly how his cheeks would be sucked in just a little, the tightness of the lines around his golden eyes. If there wasn't the full distance of the canoe between us, I might have crawled forward then, to hug him or swat some sense into him, I wasn't sure which. But it would be dangerous now, even in the flat water, to try to make my way to him.

When Gordon had his line in, he cast out again, quartering upstream expertly. I doubted he'd forgotten a thing, no matter what he said. I began casting too, pulling my line in whenever we reached a bend I'd have to steer through. We both started to catch fish, and I saved a few for Sandy.

The day never did warm the way it should have, and when we stopped for lunch I started a little fire. While I was building it up, when it still needed my help to keep burning, Gordon fished the hole just upstream. The glaze-thin ice had never melted off, and though there was no sun, the ice glinted white at the edge of the riffles, where the water did not move fast enough to break it.

Gordon worked the riffles, bouncing his nymph along the bottom through the broken water. I watched him pick up a fish with his first cast, then I went back to working on the fire. The next time I looked he had another fish on. His breath smoked into the pinching air.

When the fire had taken hold I sat beside it to watch Gordon fish. I studied him a long time, trying again to picture the sullen look of a hatred we'd never understood—the look I'd thought was directed at me for replacing his father, that Sandy had thought was for her ever divorcing in the first place. He was intent on his fishing, and he kept at it a long while without turning to see that he was being watched. He seemed to have worked the hold out, though, and he didn't hook anything else.

Maybe it was the overcast, blocking the arc of the sun, that hid the slipping away of the day, but I sat by that fire far too long watching Gordon, while the day—and our light—kept getting shorter, the river still stretching out before us.

Finally he reeled his line in and walked back to the fire, draping three trout over the log I was sitting on. "Let's eat," he said.

He caught me looking at the dead fish and he said, "You've killed three too. Now you can save them for Mom. She loves them."

I couldn't tell if the fish were a peace offering or if he was making fun of my murderous ways. I told him we'd save his for his mom, and I picked up my beautifully clean little trout, and we roasted them straight over coals we dragged from the main body of the fire. We ate with our fingers, and Gordon said he hadn't tasted anything like that in years. Even then, when I knew we had to get moving, we stayed over the fire, unable to draw away from its warmth, from the mesmerizing dance of the flames.

As Gordon watched the fire, I finally asked the question neither Sandy nor I had been able to manage the night before. After all, we were on the river now, and there was no place he could run. "What brings you back, Gordon?" I whispered.

Gordon didn't look up from the fire. For a long time he didn't answer. "Monique, I guess. She started it, anyway." He looked up then and smiled for a moment. "I'm glad she did, though. Some things get to seem way harder than they really are."

Somehow that shy little smile did all the wrong things, and the urge to reach across the fire and wipe it off his mouth welled up. "Six years is an awful long time," I said. "Without a word."

Gordon nodded and looked back into the last of the flames. "I know."

"We didn't even know if you were still alive. You about killed Sandy."

Gordon nodded again, a quick, guilty dip of his head. "When I left I thought that's what she was doing to me."

I looked away from him then, and when neither of us could say any more, I walked down to the canoe for the bailing bucket. I filled it in the river and came back to douse the fire.

"We're late," I said, too fast, trying to cut him off before he could say anything else. "We stayed here too long."

"How much farther do we have to go?"

"A long way."

The water hit the fire with a screaming hiss, and great clouds of steam poured up, mixing with the leaden sky. Gordon stirred the ashes with a stick, and I poured on a second bucket. "It's dead now," he said.

"We've got to move, Gordon. We're going to have a hell of a time making it home before dark."

He nodded but stood still over the blackened sticks, watching the last of the steam trickling up. "That's what Mom always used to say. Remember that? 'Be sure to be home before dark.'"

I nodded. "She never said it much to me," I said.

"She didn't have to," he started, but before he said anything else, he pointed into the sky. "More geese."

I looked up at the tired, ragged Vs, low with the clouds. "Looking for a place to go spend the night," I said.

"Already heading south?"

"It's getting that late. So are we."

"They sound sad to be leaving," Gordon said, walking to the canoe.

I held the canoe steady in the current while he climbed in. I pushed off and started paddling. "We really are late," I told him. "We've got to move."

Gordon picked up his paddle and started to put his back into it. I made some comment about his strength, and he started in on what his workout schedule was and all that. It was exactly the kind of mindless, friendless chitchat I'd been afraid of miring down in all day.

But Gordon stopped in mid-sentence, as if he'd been thinking the same thing. "Do both the geese raise their young? The male and the female?" he asked.

I opened my mouth to answer, but then guessed it really wasn't a question so much. "I don't know," I lied, and we both paddled hard, watching the clouds, dropping even lower, hiding the mountains the sun was setting behind.

We kept up the power as dusk wrapped around us, working too hard to speak. And then the snow began to fall, tiny white touches against our faces. "Warm enough?" I asked, and Gordon said he was fine. The snow grew steadily, patient at its task, bringing on the dark even more quickly.

"Are we going to get out of here before dark?" Gordon asked.

"Not a chance," I answered, thinking of Sandy watching the snow and the clock.

"What are we going to do?"

"Keep going, I guess. The river's pretty easy." But I followed the river's curves in my mind, through the looping S just before the takeout. I told Gordon about it. "There are three snags in it. Upstream one in the center, next one left, last one right. It's not hard in the light."

"Can we reach it before dark?"

"I don't know." I felt the canoe push forward a little harder with Gordon's next stroke, and I put my back into my own paddling. I knew we wouldn't make it.

Our eyes kept searching through less and less light, until finally we were guessing at shadows. Soon I realized I was listening for the bank more than trying to see it.

We both stopped paddling for a moment. "Should we get out and walk?" Gordon asked.

"I don't have a light," I said, trying to remember if I'd ever forgotten to bring one before. "We'd probably get lost. At least I know where the river goes."

I could hear Gordon cut his wooden blade into the water, and he began to paddle again, my ears straining against the blinding darkness.

"Is this dumb?" Gordon asked. "Are we going to kill ourselves out here tonight?"

"Of course it's dumb."

"I knew it would be," he said, but then I began to hear the faint rise in the hissing of the water. I said, "We may be there." I reached out my paddle and it touched against the bank.

Gordon said, "The snags?"

The hiss was a rushing sound now, and I said, "Yes. If you can see the first one, go hard left after it."

"I can't see a thing."

"Well, hear. If you can hear it."

We were quiet then, and the rushing grew louder. It seemed to be in the right place. I held my paddle out to the bank once more, measuring, remembering the snags. The blade scraped harshly against the gravel, and the air around us erupted.

The explosion of honking startled me so badly it was a moment before I realized it was geese, hundreds of them, struggling up from the banks. The wind whistled and whisked through their wings. Their honking battered my ears, as if they screamed warnings, unable to believe I couldn't hear. I thought if I reached up perhaps they would lift me off this river, over the snags ahead.

I felt Gordon pulling hard to the left and, though I could hear nothing but the geese, I drew hard that way. Then the canoe brushed something on the right, lifting and listing, and I thought we were going over. There was a flash of lighter water on that side and the canoe righted itself and we were through before I knew we'd started. The geese and the rush of water faded behind us, and I could hear Gordon breathing hard up front.

"Did we make it?" he whispered. "Were those the snags?"

"Those were the snags."

"We hit the last one, didn't we?"

"Grazed it."

"Are there any more? Was that the last of it?"

"That's all," I said, my heart only now beginning to speed up, battering at my ribs as I pictured the two of us tumbling alone through the black, ice-bound current.

Gordon said something else, but we broke through another flock of geese. They sounded as if they were in the boat, and I could feel individual birds going over my head. Once I heard the hard flutter of braking wings, and a heavy gust of air hit my cheek. When they faded downstream, Gordon said, "One of them touched me. On the face."

"I thought they were going to carry us away."

"What will they do now? How will they land in the dark?"

"I don't know."

"They don't have to keep flying until it gets light, do they?"

He sounded so distressed I said, "No." though I didn't have any idea what they could or could not do. "They can land at night. They can feel how close they are to the ground."

"Really?" he asked, and I said, "Sure."

"I wish I could've done that," he said, and we kept moving down-river, occasionally touching the banks with our paddles to make sure we were still there. Gordon said it was like floating through space, and if he couldn't touch the bank, he wouldn't even know he was on the planet. "Maybe we didn't make it through the snags. Maybe this is our afterlife."

"No," I said. "We wouldn't be here without your mom. I wouldn't be."

"Or Monique. Monique would be with me."

I waited for him to say, "And Mom," but he didn't do that. I said, "What did you think about when we started to tip back there? Who did you think about?"

"Monique," he answered, too fast, before he could have given it any thought. Then he blurted. "She's pregnant. That's what I thought about. That's why she made me come here to see Mom."

I didn't say anything. I'd wanted him to say he thought about Sandy, but I could see now why that wouldn't be true.

Then Gordon said, "That's all I ever think about now. I walk around scared to death. Scared about things I'd never even thought of."

I laughed a little, vengefully, but Gordon ignored me. "Does that ever leave? Even when you've taken all the tests? Even when you know the baby is all right? Isn't the fear supposed to go away?"

The moon had come up behind the clouds, and I could see the faint-est outline of Gordon against the sky. I told him that the fear goes away, although I really don't know much about it. Gordon was my only experi-ence at being a parent, and he'd been 10 years old when we'd met. But I remembered getting up on nights as dark as this to stand in his doorway, listening for his breathing, and I doubted that the fear ever disappeared completely. No test was that foolproof.

"Why won't mine go away, then? My fear?"

"Maybe it changes more than goes away. Becomes more awe than fear."

"Just the thought of being a dad scares me," Gordon whispered. "What if you do your best and they turn out like me?"

There was no answer for that, and we paddled until suddenly the take-out was there, appearing as quickly as the water cut by the snags. I pulled over, and the canoe scraped the gravel, and I said "End of the line."

Gordon stayed in his seat. I could see his outline in the river now, the water holding the light of the clouds. I held my hand out. I don't know how he saw it in the dark, but he took it and I pulled him up out of the canoe. Once he was on the bank, we let go of each other.

"We've got to move. We're probably scaring Sandy to death."

We picked up the canoe and carried it toward my truck. "Does she worry about you now? Does she tell you to be home before dark?" Gordon asked.

"Of course," I said. "She loves me."

"So there's nothing left for you to fear, is there?"

"Losing that."

"Doesn't that scare you to death? All by itself?"

"No," I said, wondering if that was true. "You can't start missing the greatest thing in the world before it's even gone." I paused, trying to remember his words. "You'd wind up crazy if you did that."

We lifted the canoe onto the truck, and when I walked around for the tie-downs I bumped into Gordon in the dark. I felt the sticky touch of the fish he'd killed for his mother. He stepped quickly backward and I could feel him staring at me. "She'll love those fish," I said.

"I'm sorry," he said. "About leaving. About everything. I was such a mess then."

His words brushed against my face like the startled rush of a goose wing. I told him that his mother had known that all along, but if he could bring himself to tell her, it would be like one of those wondrous tests they had now, the ones Monique had taken, that really assured nothing but meant so much anyway.

take two

Scott Waldie

Warren objected strongly to his condition being described as merely "brokenhearted"; Maggie's leaving had hollowed him out body and limb. Sometimes, and he was sure the booze wasn't helping, he felt as though he were nothing but eyeballs and skin. Maggie had been gone for two years. The first year he buried himself in work, the second year he buried himself in the bottle. And, he was confident, if he continued with the insane hours and the martinis, this year's burial would be in a box.

His need for a vacation had become even more apparent to his co-workers at Ogilvy & Mather. In fact, if it weren't for them he wouldn't be bumping his way down this Montana back road. The art department had pooled their money for his 40th birthday and bought him a new fly rod and an airplane ticket. This, he was sure, was done more for their sanity than for his. Being the creative director of a New York ad agency is enough to make any man edgy, but he had gone three years without any time off, and it was turning him into a full-fledged asshole.

Warren unfolded the directions given him back at the tackle shop in the last small town of Travers Corners. This was not the kind of country in which you would want to miss any turns. He had not seen a soul since leaving the main highway an hour ago. But he was on course—there was the abandoned homestead and windmill. All he had to do was turn right at the next fork.

It was hot and still. In the mirror his dust lay motionless over miles of straight road. Up ahead it was changing: The valley was narrowing, the sagebrush and parched grasses swept quickly now into rock cliffs and, above those, the forest. Tumbleweeds and the skeletal remains of blue-green sage were piled up against barbed-wire fences, and cattle huddled around the watering holes.

At the fork he stopped and got out of the car. At his feet, half-buried in the grass and leaning against a fence post, was a sign with two arrows pointing in opposite directions. After one arrow it read, "Emmett Spoons —three miles" and after the other, "Missoula—114 miles." It was light years away from his usual crossroads of 48th Street and Fifth Avenue and the faceless swarms of the yup-and-coming. No horns. No taxis. Nobody sleeping in the doorways. No doorways. Nobody. He had seen one rattle-snake coiled at the side of the road and a couple of coyotes skulking through the brush, so at least the inside traders were represented.

He turned right on to the Emmett Spoons fork and after the first bend he suddenly traded the high mountain desert for a lush meadow and the glint of running water—the South Fork of the Elkheart River.

A log cabin stood at the edge of the stream, just as his directions read. Out front an old man was turned away from him, chopping wood.

Warren shouted his first hello before leaving the car, but he wasn't heard. As he walked closer, past a vegetable garden and an old pickup, he tried another greeting; still no response. The old man was tall and bent and moved like a rusted marionette. A great shock of white hair struggled against his straw hat. And, in spite of the heat, he wore a ragged gray sweater; his shirt showed through at the elbows.

Warren was nearly up to the old man before he became aware of his presence, and it gave the old timer quite a start. "Sweet Jesus Marie," he said, recoiling slightly from the surprise, "what are you trying to do, scare what little life I have left outta me?"

"I'm sorry Mister Spoons. I said hello a couple of times, but you didn't hear me."

"Hearin's not so good anymore. Who the hell are you?"

"My name is Warren Smith. The guy down at the fishing store back in Travers Corners said that you might let me fish your river." He'd also mentioned that Emmett Spoons was a cantankerous old fart and that he was to tread lightly while asking.

"Ain't my river, it's God's river. But it's my land and you can't fish the crick unless you trespass. Last fella I let fish left a big mess, so I don't know."

Warren felt an urgent need to strike a bargain. "I could work a trade. Maybe I could split some wood for you. I haven't done it since I was a kid."

"Where you from?"

"New York."

"Well, let me tell you something, New York. You're still a kid. I'm 74 years old and I been splitting wood since birth, so it's kinda lost some of its originality. So you just made yourself a trade." He handed Warren the ax. "Have at 'er, Smitty. Hope you don't mind me calling you Smitty. Knew a Smith once. Called him Smitty. You kinda remind me of him."

Warren stripped off his shirt. He was thin and made doubly pale by being redheaded. His arms looked like vanilla buggy whips, which didn't surprise him, for Magic Markers were about the heaviest thing he'd lifted in years. His legs were in good shape, though, for he walked everywhere in Manhattan—that is, everywhere his schedule didn't make him run.

He split logs for several hours and barely put a dent in Emmett's woodpile. He liked the Zen of splitting wood: balancing the log on the stump, aligning its weakest crease to the fall of the ax, the crack of the wood, and the burst of pine smell rushing his senses. He stood evicted from his every day. No phones. No storyboards.

Sweat rolled down his spine and soaked the waist of his Levi's. Periodically he would shake the sweat from his hair and walk over to the small irrigation ditch that fed Emmett's garden to splash cool water on his face.

Emmett worked in the garden for a time, then went inside. He was back now by the creek, lifting a large wooden bucket from the water. "Hey, Smitty," he called and waved him over.

Warren laid down his ax and brushed the pine chips from his pants. He slipped on his shirt, rolled up the sleeves, but left it unbuttoned. The muscles that hadn't atrophied in his arms and shoulders were pumped hard. He felt the beginnings of blisters on his palms but imagined them to be calluses. He wanted to light up a Camel. He wanted to slick his hair back and ease a Stetson into place. He wanted to walk up to the camera and drawl, "Only one kind of soap can get these hands clean, mister—Lava."

Warren sensed a slight swagger to his step as he crossed the yard. There are varying degrees of John Wayne in all men, but New York City is much too cosmopolitan to allow any swaggering. Pin-striped strutters, however, are commonplace.

Emmett pulled a couple of beers from the bucket and handed one to Warren. "Lectricity couldn't of gotten them any colder."

"Nope."

"Phone?"

"Nope. Tryin' to keep things simple. I was always pound-foolish with my money, and Social Security don't stretch far enough to cover all the luxuries. Anyway, I'd rather have a cold beer than a phone call from my sister. Now get inside. I built some sandwiches."

Inside the cabin was much different from what Warren had expected. It was all one room. One wall was stocked with jars of preserves, and the others were covered with black-and-white photographs. They were mostly group pictures, and at first glance they appeared to be of ranch hands. But on the third photo he got no farther than the first two guys from the left: Bing Crosby and Fred MacMurray.

Emmett looked up and caught Warren gawking. "Picture above that one has Gary Cooper in it. Taken in nineteen hundred and thirty-five."

"Yeah, and Guy Kibbee and Victor McLaglen."

"You like the old movies?" asked Emmett.

Warren briefly explained about his love affair with the movies, especially those from the '30s and '40s. And how his Saturday afternoons were typically spent at the Biograph Cinema on West 57th, watching Bogart sneer and lisp his way through an old two-reeler, or taking in *Citizen Kane* for the twelfth time.

Then he went back to identifying the stars, calling out their names as he recognized them, like a tourist in Sardi's: "Gable, Lombard, William Frawley, Wallace Beery. Where did you get these photographs? They're wonderful."

"See that big gawkin' kid standing next to Bing?"

"Yeah."

"That's me."

Over lunch Emmett chronicled the old photographs, as well as his own past and the history of the Snowbound Ranch. Not all in that order. It was just that one history couldn't unfold without the other two. From the late '20s until his death, the Snowbound was owned by the famous film director Charles Gilbert. Emmett never married.

"I was born on the Snowbound. My mother wrestled pots and my father ramrodded the outfit. One hundred'n forty thousand acres. When it came time for my old man to step down, I sorta stepped in, and I was her foreman till ten years ago. When Gilbert died, he left me this cabin and a quarter-section."

The afternoon flew by. Emmett was a natural storyteller, with his rich Montana accent and attention to detail. The stories were better than the best double bill. Warren didn't know whether he should ask questions or just be dandled on the old man's knee.

The alarm on Warren's watch beeped. In New York, it was time to head home.

"What the hell was that?" Emmett asked.

"My watch."

"Is it broke?"

"No," Warren laughed, "just the alarm." It put him in touch with the actual time. "I'd better go set up my camp."

Emmett followed Warren to the door. On the wall by the door hung the photograph of a beautiful woman, and it stopped Warren short. Publicity photos of actresses from the '30s, although glamorous, were fairly standardized. Typically, the women were photographed under diffused but dramatic lighting and, whether they were vamps, sirens, or girls next door, they came off as porcelain creatures staring at something desirous but unattainable just off camera.

But not the woman in this picture. It was a studio portrait: Columbia's name appeared in the corner of the frame. This woman stared into a very close camera as if she were capturing its soul. Her dark hair flowed to the edges of the photograph, and she had a look that fell somewhere between witchery and bold innocence. Was the full mouth the enticement of a temptress or the pout of a child? And her eyes! They were light and burned through that old duotone as if the world held but two colors and her eyes held the rest.

"Who is she?" Warren asked.

"Molly Horn. She wasn't a big star. Only made a few pictures."

"I think," Warren paused and squinted into his own archives, "I think I remember her. Wasn't she in that comedy with Spencer Tracy and Claudette Colbert? What was the name of tha . . . ?"

"*Separate Lives*," Emmett answered.

"Yeah, right, right. She played the bootlegger's daughter. The wedding scene is cinema history. She was incredibly funny."

Emmett was visibly pleased, with an almost fatherly pride, that Warren knew of her. "Smitty, you know your movies. Molly stole every scene she was in. No easy trick against the likes of Tracy and Colbert. She could act circles around any of 'em. Why she could have been the biggest star that ever was. And it wasn't just my opinion, neither. Charles Gilbert knew it. Cooper knew it. Hell, anybody that ever saw her act knew it." Emmett grew more animated with every word; his brown eyes caught fire and glowed over his high cheekbones. "You're probably wondering what an ol' fool from the Elkheart Mountains knows about Hollywood. Well, every summer the Snowbound was Hollywood, especially the summer of '37 and . . . ."

Warren was so taken by her beauty that he was unaware of his interruption. "What happened? Why didn't she make any more movies?"

"Listen, Smitty. It's a long story. I tell you what. You come back in a few days, and I'll burn us a couple of steaks. I'll tell you all about it then." He pointed at two large photo albums in the corner. "Got a lot more pictures to show you, too."

"I'd really like that."

On the way to Warren's car, Emmett gave directions. "Drive until you get to the end of the road. About two miles. There's a big ol' cottonwood and a good place to camp. Fishin's good up there. Just be careful of the bogs. They're almost quicksand. You step in one and you'll be up to your neck in black muck. Take you a day to work yourself out. Just don't step into any black-bottomed swampy places and you'll do just fine.

"Walked up that way last week. River sure has changed some. Cut itself some new channels this spring. Highest water we've had in 50 years this June." He slapped Warren on the back. "You know, Smitty, you look a little puny to me. Think a few days in the mountains is going to do you good. I'll see you in a couple of days."

Warren buttoned his shirt. His swagger was in no danger of returning.

Camp took several hours to set up, but everything was in place as the bats started to dart about against the twilight. The wood was gathered, the tent was pitched and his new fly rod leaned against the lone cottonwood, all strung up, poised and ready for the next morning.

The flames of his campfire grew more crimson with the oncoming darkness and projected his shadow against the cliffs. He heard the cry of a coyote. The real West. He might have lost his swagger, but for the rest of this trip he was Smitty.

Warren spent most of the following days fishing, his remaining time divided between making out shapes in the clouds and napping on the stream's grassy banks. At night he tried to decipher the stars, wondering how he, or anybody else, could piece together a moving puzzle. He also played his last day with Maggie over again. Nothing new there. Over the last few years it had become a nightly feature.

It was a regular Thursday morning. Except that morning, over coffee and bagels, Maggie announced she had been offered a promotion to the London office. And she was going to take it. Over the years it hadn't been the news that dogged him as much as her delivery. In a heartbeat she had given him the room key to limbo and invited gravity into all his dreams. And she had said it all with that icy detachment of hers, like she had just asked him to pass the cream cheese.

His attitude toward women since then had been cyclical. At times he hated women but loved Maggie. Then he would hate Maggie and try to love other women. But the other women failed because they weren't Maggie. At which point he would enter phase three, and never leave the apartment. There he would sit, on the couch where they had loved, eating at the coffee table they had refinished together, looking up at the Chagall print they had bought from their favorite gallery in Soho, until he went insane and started the cycle all over again.

His third day of fishing was proving even better than the first two. The new fly rod was a delight. Yesterday his casting was still a little on the rough side, but this afternoon the timing seemed to have finally worked its way down from his mind into his casting arm and he was setting the fly down pretty much where he pleased. He had caught and released 20 fish and missed perhaps another dozen.

The brook trout upstream in the beaver ponds hadn't been fooled a bit by this morning's attempts, but down through the meadows, the rainbow trout had been most eager. He thought of keeping a few; perhaps Emmett would enjoy them for breakfast. But killing trout ran contrary to Warren's convictions as a preservationist. It was also against his moral tenets as an angler and the cosmological formula he had adhered to since youth, that being the number of fish a fisherman killed adversely affected the fisherman's luck for the rest of his lifetime.

By the time he'd fished back to camp the sun was low and nearing the ridgeline. The pool beside the camp was darkening to an emerald green and the sun's image, reflected a thousand times in the trough and crest of each ripple, made the stream look as though it were spilling from tiffany windows. Several trout rose to snatch mayflies from the surface, but he was fished out and opted for a cold beer.

He took off his shoes and sat on the streambank, kicking divots from the current with his big toe. The effects of the beer and a long day soon had him horizontal. The sun was settling into his inner reaches, warming and loosening his flesh until it hung from his bones like bread dough. The light sifted through his closing lashes and flickered between reality and a purple haze. He thought of tonight's dinner and listening to more of Emmett's stories. If this were to be one of life's finest moments, he was glad to be making a week out of it.

The tall grass was cooling. The streamside temperature and his skin seemed to meld, and for a while it felt as if his clothes were the only bonds preventing him from dissolving into thin air. He'd known evenings such as this in New York, when he and Maggie would sit on the fire escape feeling Manhattan stabilize after a hot summer day, the heat giving way to the silky and embracing night air. They'd listen to the city's sounds and talk about the things that mattered.

He was awakened sharply by a loud splash that brought him upright. It was as if someone had thrown a large stone into the pool. He knew he wasn't dreaming, for rings were lapping against the bank and water had been sprayed on the rocks. But nothing was around. Nothing stirred. He finally had to shrug it off as a beaver that had ventured down from the ponds.

On the drive down to Emmett's, his muscles ached, and he smelled of fish and camp smoke. He had a three-day beard and was sunburned. He had lost track of the number of fish he had fooled. It was the best he'd felt in years.

Over a two-course dinner of cold beer and steaks, Emmett told story after story about the old days at the Snowbound. About Judy Garland singing at the piano, Gable's practical jokes, Gary Cooper sharing sourdough recipes with Emmett's mother.

"Charles Gilbert built himself a little theater into the main house and practically every night he'd show a movie. And there we'd all be, cowhands and cooks, rubbin' elbows with the movie stars. Watching *The Thin Man* sittin' alongside Myrna Loy and sharin' a bag of corn with William Powell. And the nearest picture show a hundred miles off in Missoula. It was quite a deal, I'm tellin' you.

"Why hell, most of them movie people were just as ordinary as other folks. Prettier than most and a little high-strung maybe, but they sure treated us decent. And if they didn't, Charles Gilbert never asked 'em back. He was like that."

Throughout dinner a summer storm began filling the sky. There was nothing gradual about the first few raindrops; they came in with the rest of the cloudburst, sending Warren and Emmett scurrying for the cabin.

Thunder, lightning, rain-streaked windows and kerosene lamplight added to the mystique of the old photographs in Emmett's albums. The first album was full of stars, their exaggerated fashions, their long cars and their antics: Henry Fonda and Jimmy Stewart draped over the fenders of a giant Packard, while Katharine Hepburn stood on the running board with a rifle slung over her shoulder; Irene Dunn fishing in an ermine stole; David Niven astride a horse that was saddled backwards. A chuckle rumbled up occasionally from somewhere deep in Emmett's past as he flipped through the pages. "Movie stars. Point a camera at 'em and they just naturally gotta do somethin'."

The second album was very different. It was all Molly Horn. Molly on horseback. Molly sitting on a tractor. Molly with Errol. Molly with Bing. Emmett's voice softened with each page, falling from that of a storyteller to the gentle ramblings of an old man.

"She was something, and I ain't just a-woofin' you. Guess I was pretty much in love with her. But I wasn't alone there. I guess about every man and Jack that ever was around Molly fell in love with her. She had some kinda magic. She'd change your life by just entering the room. She had a smile that could set you at ease. And a pair of eyes. Well, they weren't describable, that's all." Then he smiled and pointed to a bracelet on her wrist. "Always had this old piece of Egyptian jewelry on her wrist. Asked her about it one day, she just laughed, then went in to a Boris Karloff imitation and told me the bracelet gave her all her powers. She was a pistol, that one.

"Anyway, with the likes of Gable and Copper flirting with her, she wasn't likely to go for some spindly 19-year-old kid.

"Molly was a whole passel of people all rolled into one. She could talk and look like anybody. She could twist her hair one way and she was Bette Davis, twist it another and she was Tallulah Bankhead. She had so many different looks."

"Like Meryl Streep?" Warren asked.

"Who?"

"Never mind."

Emmett continued. "Everybody knew she was going to be a big star, but up until '37 she had only done a few bit parts. But that summer she got herself a starring role opposite Gary Cooper in a western called *North of Texas*. They filmed it right over on the Lark Fork near Missoula, and on weekends Gilbert would bring cast and crew to the Snowbound.

"Things couldn't have been going any better for her. She was slated to star in *Mr. Deeds Goes to Town* when the western was finished."

"I've never heard of *North of Texas*." Warren puzzled, and he was a big Cooper fan.

"Never got released."

"Why not?"

"Molly Horn disappeared."

Warren had enough What happened? written across his face that he didn't need to ask.

And Emmett answered. "That was quite a summer around here. Gary Cooper, Jean Arthur, Ronald Colman, Thomas Mitchell, Guy Kibbee, Claude Raines. Movie stars flyin' in and out.

"They finished filmin' everything they could up here in the woods. They were goin' to shoot the rest back in the studios," Emmett explained as he flipped the album to the last page, and a photograph of Molly sitting on a corral fence with a fishing rod in her hand. "This is the last picture ever taken of her. It was her last day on the ranch and she decided to get in one more day of fishin'. She was hell with a fishin' pole. Outfished

Bing one day, and he was a fair hand. Well, anyways, she went fishin'. She went alone. She never came back."

"Did she run away?"

"Murdered. Course, that never did get proved, not in a court of law anyway. Police never found her body, and it's still on the books as an accidental drowning. That was horseshit, and I knew it right from the get-go. That girl never drowned."

"Who do you think did it?"

"Don't think. I know who done it, and it didn't take no Sherlock Holmes, neither. The night before Molly was murdered, Gilbert threw a big party. It was quite a do. There was a band and dancin'. I got to dance with Molly that night. Just about the biggest thrill I ever did have. Anyways, at the party, Bill announces about *Mr. Deeds* and who's goin' to star in it."

"No small film."

"Not hardly," Emmett agreed and went on. "There was a gal, a young starlet named Isabelle Sloan. She wanted to be a star and she was screwin' the young associate producer, tryin' to get up in the business," Emmett winked. "If you know what I mean. It came out that this producer had promised the Sloan gal the part Gilbert gave to Molly.

"Now you heard of parts that actors would kill for, well, that's just what she did. She followed Molly up the river that day and killed 'er, as sure as I'm sittin' here. Then she rolled her body along with a few rocks into one of them bogs. Like I say, it never got proved, but two days later Isabelle Sloan hung herself and that sort of solved it for everybody."

"Then you're telling me that Molly Horn was murdered where I'm fishing?"

"Found her clothes by the second beaver pond."

  Undiscovered movie memorabilia to a cinemaphile is like Leakey finding an older bone, like an unknown van Gogh turning up in an attic in Queens, or getting a cab on Lexington on a rainy day. Warren's knowledge of early films fueled Emmett from one story to the next. The rain had long stopped, but lightning still sent spasms of light through the cabin. Emmett yawned.

"Say, I had better be getting back to camp." Warren said. "It's got to be getting very late."

"About three hours from sunup, I suppose."

At the door, Warren stopped to look at Molly's portrait. Lightning flashed, causing the glass in the frame to reflect against the windowpane, and for one quick and eerie moment, Molly seemed to be on the outside looking in with those eyes.

"You know, she was about the best and worst thing that ever happened to me," Emmett said, straightening her picture. "After knowing Molly, I lost the rest of my life comparing her to every other woman I met. Made for some lonely times."

Warren understood. "Hey, I'll stop by tomorrow and put another dent in that woodpile."

"Naw, you done enough. Anyways, I won't be here tomorrow. Saturdays I go to my sister's. She's crippled up with arthritis and it makes her ornerier than hell. I ain't looking forward to it none."

"Well then, guess I'll be saying my goodbye now," Warren said, shaking Emmett's hand. "I sure enjoyed my time here. The fishing was great. But, I'll be remembering this night for a long time to come. It sure was a pleasure to meet you."

"Same back at you, Smitty. And you come back any time you please."

"Oh, I have some leftover supplies that I would just as soon not have to take back on the plane."

"You can leave 'em on the kitchen table. Leave 'em outside and the varmints will get into 'em. Much obliged. Good night."

"Good night, Emmett."

Morning was grand. Everything glistened from the rainfall, and the sage smelled sweet. On his walk to the ponds he found himself whistling a nondescript New Age melody.

The wind was blowing gently when Warren reached the first pond, ruffling the surface just enough to mask his casts. The brookies were lined up to take his presentations, and the fishing was like something he had never seen before. One cast equaled one fish, or at least a strike.

Fishing the second pond was a little creepy after the previous night's story, and when the wind gusted suddenly to whip the pond's surface to a silvery finish, sending him downstream in search of more sheltered water, he was actually relieved.

All day long the wind came in fits and starts, but nothing could hurt the fishing. It was spectacular. He was giddy and at times he couldn't keep from giggling out loud. No one in Manhattan was going to believe this day of fishing.

The wind died to a dead calm just as he reached the pool next to camp. In the strong light it was hard to tell if it was a mink or a beaver swimming in the current. He crouched down and, hiding behind the lip of the bank, crept as close as possible.

He peered through the brush only to stare in disbelief. His mink, in reality, was a large rainbow trout. Bigger than anything he had seen all week. Twenty inches easy.

The trout moved contently, lolling in the current like a drunk reveling in a vat of his favorite elixir. The fish swam so shallow at times that her back breached the surface and her dorsal fin feathered through the water, sending rippling chevrons into the current. Leisurely sipping at mayflies as they floated past, she would loop and turn, rolling her rainbow, showing her sides of ruby, pearl and shell.

Warren moved carefully away from the bank and retraced his steps, until he stood in the creek well behind the feeding trout.

He false-cast his fly until it reached the needed range, then laid it down on the current. He worried that with all the naturals on the water, the fish wouldn't fall for his artificial. His heart raced.

The fly passed right over the rainbow, but she paid it no heed. He let it float. He didn't want to lift it off too quickly, for fear of spooking her. The fish turned abruptly, creating a giant boil, and smashed the fly. The river erupted. The trout flew high above the water in a rage of twisting silver.

The second jump landed her not back in the stream, but into a pile of willows and roots that shaded a corner of the pool. Writhing and thrashing, actually breaking a few of the branches, she finally made it back into the water.

He stripped in line in an effort to keep up with her moves, but when he drew taut, it was not to the trout. He jerked his rod tip a few times, only to watch a clump of willows twitch in accord. He was hopelessly entangled. The fish had vanished.

Disheartened he had missed his chance at "the big one," Warren reeled in his line, following it until he was even with his tangled fly. His hand followed the leader down into the willows. It was so lost in the brush and the mud and the moss that it was easier just to pull up everything surrounding the fly than to free the fly alone.

When he finally separated the goo from the driftwood, he found his fly wound around something heavy and metallic. He swished his find through the water and rubbed it, then scraped it with his pocketknife until the brass finish and mother-of-pearl used for making lures years ago finally shone through the mire. He stood, gave the old spoon a closer look, then dropped it into his shirt pocket. It was time to head home.

Warren broke camp, saddened that his vacation was over, and at the same time pleased with how well it had gone: the quiet, the fishing, Emmett's great stories. He felt especially fine when it dawned on him that he hadn't thought of Maggie once all day.

He stopped at Emmett's to drop off his leftover groceries. The old man was gone, as he had said he would be, and as Warren set the box of food on the table he wanted to say thanks again in a note. He patted his pockets in search of a pen, but instead found the already forgotten lure. He dropped it to the table, then searched until he located a pen. He wrote, "Emmett, thanks again for everything. Next summer the steaks and the beer are on me" and signed it "~~Warr~~ Smitty."

He paused once more at Molly's photograph, then headed for the car.

That night on the flight out of Missoula, Warren broke the pattern of people he usually drew as seat companions. Normally he ended up between two rabbis, or a couple from Des Moines returning from a Wayne Newton concert or a farm implement show. Somehow, this time, he was seated beside a most attractive brunette who was going home after a week of canoeing. Their conversation was so immediate and flirtatious that they didn't get around to introductions until somewhere over the Dakotas. "My name is Warren Smith, but my friends all call me Smitty . . . ."

Back on the South Fork of the Elkheart, Emmett slept soundly, the photo album still open, from the previous night, to Molly's last photograph. A pair of wet footprints glistened across the log floor, and on the wall above his head the shadow of two hands flickered as they pulled up his covers.

And out on the highway near the city limits of Travers Corners, a trucker had just picked up a young man hitchhiking. "Where to, young fella?" asked the driver.

The hitchhiker removed a large straw hat, and long black hair cascaded down to the seat. The anxious but delighted truck driver was looking at the most beautiful young girl he had ever seen. She pushed up the sleeves of an overly large gray sweater and was immediately occupied with the piecing together of an old bracelet made of gold and mother-of-pearl.

After a lengthy delay, she looked up as the lights of an oncoming car splashed through the cab. Her eyes had an intensity the trucker had never seen before. Then she smiled, a smile that put him at ease, and said, "Oh, I don't know. Are they still making movies in LA?"

the virtual angler

Mallory Burton

Buddy Bailey stepped into the outfitting kiosk and keyed the six options he selected whenever he fished the Yellowstone: three-millimeter neoprene waders, stream cleats, a 12-pocket vest, a nine-foot-six-inch rod, a Hardy reel and a weight-forward 6-weight line. Moments later, the boy exited the booth, a walking fiche of ancient angling history.

Zaak Walton, chronicler of sport-fishing antiquities, ducked his head in amusement at the sight of the emerging figure and lifted his hands in a gesture of surrender. "All right," he said, "but this is absolutely the last time." He took an HMD from the rack and set the helmet upon the young man's head. "It's probably a mistake to indulge you, my boy," he said, "but I dearly love to watch you fish. It's like seeing one of those old-fashioned angling videos come to life. Magic to an old man's eyes!"

The boy stepped into the Wadepool, selected a freestone bottom and increased the water volume to 8,000 cubic feet per second.

Zaak frowned. "That's pretty heavy water," he said. "Sure you want it that extreme?" Buddy nodded. Zaak turned to the game console. "Activating rod," he announced.

Buddy held the rod close to his side, raised his arm and began moving the rod slowly back and forth, ten o'clock to two o'clock, establishing a rhythm. A thin beam of light shot up the length of the rod, leveling out at its tip and extending in length with each movement of the rod.

"Looks good," said Zaak. "Ready?"

"Ready," answered the boy.

Welcome to the Yellowstone, said the Ghille's synthesized voice.

Buddy turned his head to the left and, downstream, the yellow rhyolite cliffs of the canyon came rapidly into focus. He turned his head sharply to the right, and had a moment of dizziness as his gaze shot over the tumbling water to register the change of scene. From the observation platform above, Zaak saw the boy stumble momentarily in the churning pool and then regain his footing.

Buddy scanned the river in front of him, focusing on a large boulder across and slightly downstream. "Query trout," he instructed.

Affirmative, came the reply.

"Show me," said Buddy.

Top and side views of the cutthroat flashed in rapid succession across the LCD. A schematic of the fish's location plotted its holding space six centimeters behind and 17 centimeters right of rock center.

"Proceed," said the boy.

Select fly. For hint, use query mode.

Buddy's hand moved automatically to the simulated sheepskin patch on his vest, and he touched the third synthetic fly from the left.

Royal Wuff, size 10. Cast or move on.

Zaak watched as Buddy raised the rod and lengthened the laser line with a series of false-casts. The beam hovered just above the boiling surface of the wave pool, angling downstream.

Good cast. Drift average.

Buddy made a circling motion with the rod and the beam curved into a loop and jumped a short distance upstream.

Full mend. Drift upgraded.

Buddy's arm shot up, and the beam angled straight down to the water.

Fish on. Tight line.

Inside the helmet, the reel sounded in Buddy's ears, and he smiled to himself. *I like the English reels,* he thought. *They have the best effects.*

Into the backing. Advise drag.

In response, Buddy palmed the reel. Eventually the fish slowed.

End run.

Buddy reeled in the cutthroat. Three icons blinked before him on the screen.

Weigh holograph or terminate? asked the Ghille.

"Release fish," said Buddy. Zaak leaned over the rail of the observation platform.

Fish release strictly prohibited by federal regulation 1126B, pursuant to the Animal Rights Act of the year 2020.

Buddy stretched his arms out and lowered them into the water.

Illegal act. Authorities notified. System shutting down.

Zaak put his head in his hands.

The boy tore off the HMD and clambered out of the pool. "What happened?" he asked.

"You heard the Ghille. It's illegal to release fish. The virtual angling games are hooked up directly to the Wildlife Division."

"It's a game!"

"Gamers are subject to the same ethics restrictions as citizens are. You know that."

"Yes, sir," said the boy. He looked down at the floor in an attempt to conceal his excitement. After he had released the fish, before the program had shut down, he had seen the fish swim away. The original program must have contained a loop for fish release.

"Fortunately you have an impressive record of terminations to date . . . 180 fish last week alone. I think I can get you out of it with some counseling, but you'd better let me handle it. Go home."

Zaak turned back to the terminal and initiated the program rebuild. Buddy entered the outfitting kiosk, dissolved his gear and keyed his home designations. Zaak frowned and bent over the monitor.

"Dammit!" he said. "We've lost the program."

Following the protocol designed to avoid the embarrassment of a directed visit, Zaak Walton issued an official invitation to his superior, and moments later Dory Roosevelt, senior wildlife manager, occupied Zaak's visitation chair. She entered the briefing mode and was acquainted instantly with the details of the incident.

"I see," she said. "Would you recommend the boy's exclusion from the virtual angling program then?"

"I would hope not. He's our most promising prospect. Last week, for example, he had a perfect score on Beaverhead—Streamer Level—and a 50-fish day on Henry's Fork."

The manager cleared her throat and looked Zaak directly in the eye. "Nobody has a 50-fish day on Henry's Fork," she said.

"Buddy did. Midge Level. And half of his fish were over 20 inches."

"I see," she said. "Well, if the boy is that good, why isn't he involved with something that at least has decent graphics? Firehold, for instance. Why does he waste his time on a primitive archival program like Yellowstone? It's second-generation reality, at best."

"The young man has a sentimental and perhaps a genetic attachment. His ancestors fished extensively in the park."

"Is counseling your recommendation then?" she proceeded.

"Yes, and public hours to be carried out under my supervision."

"But he has destroyed an irreplaceable program."

"Not in its entirety. I've managed to recover the technical aspects of the game, the equipment functions and the fishing parameters. The scenery is retrievable from the archives. Only the fish are lost. Oddly enough, they're missing from the backups, too."

Ms. Roosevelt made a note to order a trace on the artificial intelligence component. Perhaps it was developing some ideas of its own on the subject of fishing. "Surely we have other cutthroat sequences," she said.

"Yes, but the Yellowstone cutts are distinctive. The substitution would not hold up to the scrutiny of an authentification panel."

"I remind you that we have a responsibility to the citizenry to preserve Yellowstone Archival Park exactly as it was passed down to us."

"I am fully aware of our responsibilities," said Zaak. He hesitated. "That's why I want to take Buddy into the park with me to reproduce the game. That would give him an opportunity to make full restitution."

The woman rose from her chair and leaned over Zaak's console. Behind her gold-rimmed optics, her eyes flashed. "Out of the question. The Purists would have our heads. The park has been closed to the general citizenry for more than a century. I might consider letting you go, but he's a minor. The park is crawling with life forms, and there's no climate control out there. The insurance liability would be outrageous."

"Frankly, Ms. Roosevelt, he's the only one who can do it."

"Oh really, Mr. Walton. And were you not genetically selected, enhanced and educated to know everything there is to know about fishing from the publication of your esteemed ancestor's book in 1653 right up to the end of outdoor angling in 2093?"

"I was, indeed, and it is widely known that my ancestor wrote an early book on fishing. But with all due respect, may I point out that the first book on fly-fishing was written by Dame Juliana Berners, in the fifteenth century. My ancestor was a bait fisherman, Ms. Roosevelt, and the fly-fishing sections in his treatise were written by a friend."

The Purists insisted on the smallest possible production crew. They were adamant that the party be teletransported directly to the site, avoiding the thermal areas, and the expedition's insurers were quick to agree. The animal rights people took a hard line at first, but eventually agreed to a strict limit of 10 replacement fish, taken from the same locations as in the original production. They also granted a permit for the filming of any wildlife that wandered accidentally into the scenery, reminding the petitioners that the park's animals had already endured centuries of hunting, fishing, species-inappropriate feeding, disruption of habitat, photographing, bird-watching and other appalling invasions of privacy under the protection of the so-called conservationists. Zaak produced a picture from the park's collection showing a primitive conveyance with its doors peeled completely away by *Ursus horrilis*, and the expedition was reluctantly granted permission to carry a tranquilizing gun to be used only in the most dire emergency. To no one's surprise, Ms. Roosevelt volunteered to take charge of the gun, and, somewhat apologetically, produced the genetic credentials necessary for the large-weapon handling. In the end, the expedition consisted of Ms. Roosevelt, Zaak Walton, Buddy Bailey and a production crew of three.

Buddy joined the others at the park's symbolic gate at 1400, wearing a colorful hoverboarder jacket and helmet in addition to the regulation park uniform he had been issued. "My mother insisted," he shrugged, entering the pre-transporting inspection area. He indicated his parent, who stood smiling nervously and waving from the adjacent security paddock.

"We specified forest green," said the Purist representative.

"It's not such a bad idea," interrupted the expedition's insurance agent. "Those jackets are rated for falls at speeds of up to 100 kilometers per hour. Besides, it'll look bad if we override a parent's specifications and there's a claim."

"Empty your pockets," demanded the Purist.

"He's a teenager," said Zaak. "Ten to one he's got food in there."

Buddy reached into his pocket and grinning, produced a handful of Mars bars. "Imported," he said. Then he reached into another pocket and extracted a small book. "I'm bringing this too." It was a reproduction of a fishing journal. "Family archives," he said. "This one's about the park."

He handed the journal to the head chronicler, and Zaak turned a few pages reverently. Ms. Roosevelt passed her hand over the entry post and keyed in the coordinates Zaak had given her. The symbolic gate opened.

"Are you going to stand there reading, or do you want to go fishing?" she asked. The Purist blanched.

"Beam me up, Scottie," said Zaak, and the group members entered the transporting cubicle in single file.

They were conveyed instantly to their destination. Buddy recognized the landscape at once. All around, the yellow lava cliffs of the canyon rose up sharply from the water's edge. Across and slightly downstream, a large boulder emerged from the churning water.

"No way," said Ms. Roosevelt.

"Give me a reading on the water volume," Zaak said to the parameters technician.

The man aimed a remote at the river. "Four thousand cubic feet per second," he answered.

"Too risky," said Ms. Roosevelt.

"He can handle it," said Zaak. "He was wading 8,000 when he blew up the game. Get into your waders," he said to Buddy, "and don't forget the stream cleats. Ms. Roosevelt," he said, "if you have concerns about our safety, perhaps you could direct them more constructively toward the creature up there."

The senior wildlife manager pivoted and scanned the cliff above. The large cat's tawny coat blended in well with the overhanging ledge, and its location was not immediately apparent. When she saw the creature, Ms. Roosevelt reached silently for the tranquilizing gun.

"Look at the claws on that thing," she said. "Maybe we should have gone to Buffalo Ford. Bison may have horns, but at least they're not carnivorous."

"If we don't have any luck here, we may have to go to Buffalo Ford," said Zaak.

The crew finished taking its readings. "We're ready to go when you are!" the director yelled. The manager looked nervously at the cat, which lifted its head at the sound of the human's voice and then went back to licking its paws.

Buddy had finished suiting up and was busily rigging a graphite rod. Zaak chose a size 10 Royal Wulff from the box of synthetics and carried it over to him. "I'd rather use this one," said the boy. He opened his fist, and Zaak picked up the fly.

"Peacock herl, calf tail and elk hair," he said. "Those are restricted materials. Where did you get this?"

Buddy shrugged.

"Don't let Roosevelt get her hands on it," said Zaak. "Do you know how to tie it on?"

Buddy rolled his eyes, knotted on the fly and stepped into the water. He waded carefully into position across from the boulder. "Query fish?" he hollered over the sound of the water.

"Better be," breathed Zaak. "Activate rod!" he called.

Buddy held the rod close to his side, raised his arm and began moving the rod slowly back and forth, establishing the same rhythm as when he had fished the Wadepool. Then he began to strip handfuls of line from the reel. The line shot up through the guides and the length of his back-cast grew. He set the line down on the water, well ahead of the boulder, mending upstream with a quick flip of his wrist. The fly drifted into and around the boulder, bumping against its water-smoothed surface. A large cutthroat rose without hesitation from behind the boulder, turned and took the fly down with him.

"Fish on!" yelled Buddy. The fish ran and Buddy palmed the reel. He followed the fish a short distance downstream and netted him in a quiet backwater. He handed the fish to the parameters technician, who quickly dispatched the cutt and sealed it in a black plastic tote.

"We got it all," said the director. "Let's do it again."

They were in the middle of the tenth sequence when the storm moved in. The shooting had run well into late afternoon, and they had mistaken the slow darkening of the sky for the setting of the sun. If anything, the disappearance of the sun had been connected with a noticeable improvement in the fishing, and Buddy was standing, midstream, playing a fish, when the crew found themselves suddenly pelted by a freezing rain. The downpour of sleet was followed almost immediately by a flash of blue light and a tumultuous roar.

"What is it?" yelled the director.

"Lightning!" shouted Zaak. "Electrical disturbance!"

"Will it interfere with the lasers?"

"Don't think so!"

"We'll finish up then! This is the last fish, and I'd like to get these effects on ROM. Okay, Ms. Roosevelt?"

She signaled her approval, and the members on the bank struggled into their waterproofs. The light and the noise were unpleasant, but there was no immediate danger. Still, it was her responsibility. "Just stay within the 50-meter radius!" she cautioned. "If anything happens, I'll E-vac us out of here, and I don't want anybody left behind. Do you hear me?"

The director nodded and turned back to his console. The technician elevated him to his previous position above the water. The chair was suddenly outlined in blue. A ball of lightning rolled down the extension and across the water. Zaak saw Buddy turn and submerge himself in the water, holding the rod high above his head. The current swept him away.

"Buddy!" Zaak staggered to the undercut riverbank and disappeared over the edge.

Ms. Roosevelt fumbled for her transmitter and pressed the E-vac button. They were back in the transporting cubicle; herself, the parameters technician, the film technician and the director, badly burned. She vomited.

The storm abated as quickly as it had arisen and the sun reappeared, though its evening rays were short-lived. They had drifted clear of the canyon and into a grassland plain, where the river widened and flowed more gently. Buddy removed his helmet and spread his jacket on the bank. With a pocketblade, he slit the outer sleeve and extracted a packet from the compartment where the elbow-protection disk should have been. He set the packet on the ground some 10 meters away, punctured the seal and stepped back. The shelter inflated and leveled itself. The site was perfect. Buddy slit the other sleeve and retrieved a sleepsac.

"Just one," he said. "We'll have to stick to the lower elevations. Sorry about that, Mr. Walton, but I never figured you'd want to come too."

He glanced at Zaak, sitting beside him on the riverbank. The old man hadn't spoken yet, but he would come around once the shock reversal took hold. Buddy made a sweeping motion in the air and held his clenched fist in front of Zaak's face. He opened the hand slowly, revealing a small brownish insect, its tent-like wings folded over its body.

"Caddis," he said. "Not many yet, but in another half-hour I figure we'll have ourselves a pretty decent hatch."

The boy picked up his jacket and emptied the pockets. He dropped the fishing journal into Zaak's lap and carried the nutritional and medical supplies over to the shelter. The sun went off the water. Buddy rigged the rod and tied on an Elkhair Caddis. The fish began to show themselves.

"The way I see it, Mr. Walton, between us we know just about everything there is know about fishing. I'll bet there's not a fish in the park that we can't catch. That journal there is full of stories about the good old days, when there were plenty of fish to go around, and big ones, too. I figure a hundred years is long enough to bring a river back, don't you?"

Zaak rose to his knees. Clouds of caddisflies swarmed on the banks, and fish slashed noisily across the surface of the water. Zaak nodded his head.

"Welcome to the Yellowstone, Mr. Walton," said Buddy. He took the man's arm and helped him to his feet. "Are you gonna be all right? We can't stay here long, you know. This is the first place they'll look."

"I'll be just fine after a bit," said Zaak. He let go of Buddy's arm and took a few tentative steps on his own. "As the Compleat Angler himself pointed out, Providence has a way of watching over us fisherfolk. Now quit your yakking, my boy. Be quiet! Be quiet; and go a-angling."

ephemerella

E. Donnall Thomas, Jr.

June 17. Blue-Wing Olives. Seven browns, three rainbows.
Water temperature: 68 degrees.

Bad day at Black Rock. I woke up too early to fish, too early to do anything but think. The thinking soon turned into brooding, and I walked out onto the porch in my underwear to try to get away from the darkness it brought along. Beyond the cabin door, the morning lay still and calm, with a heavy layer of dew glistening upon the new grass. None of this mattered in the least, not to me anyway, not this morning.

I made myself make breakfast, as if this deliberate task might have therapeutic value. My mother always believed in the healing power of food. "Eat," I can still hear her saying. "How are you going to get better if you don't eat? Just look at you," et cetera. Of course, she would have cooked with authority, which is what makes that kind of thing work. I, on the other than, wasn't fooling anybody.

But I got out the cast-iron skillet and made breakfast anyway. When the food was done, it lay there on the plate like a curse; two eggs, over easy, awash in their own slime, yellow eyes staring stupidly upward beneath a crown of turgid sausages. I sat and stared back until the familiar gorge began to rise in my throat and my upper lip started to quiver, and then I pushed the chair back and fled. I would have fed the whole damn mess to the dog if I had one.

I'm down at the creek now, listening to it babble on like a stuck record. The sun has risen in the east, proving once again that there are certain things that you can rely on even in a world as duplicitous as this one. Caddis flies are starting to stir out on the water, arousing my own instincts right along with theirs. "Let's do it," I announce to absolutely no one. The words sound reassuringly tough at first and then I remember: That's what Gary Gilmore said when they strapped him down in front of the firing squad.

By the time I get through with the preliminaries—it all seems to take so long these day—*Baetis* are coming off the water in steady swarms. Blue-wing olives, a blue-collar mayfly if there ever was one, but this is no time to stand on ceremony. Tie on a no-hackle dun; wade out into the water and begin to cast.

At first, the water itself is more interesting than the fish. The cool fluid works its way up past my knees as I wade deeper and deeper, and then it is all the way up to my crotch and I find myself regretting the efficiency of the waders. What would it be like to come right out of them, to feel the water itself against my skin, to determine once and for all whether there are any responses left there to evoke?

We will never know, for at this point the feather dun vanishes in a slurping boil and the bamboo rod—the conduit that connects me to the creek and all things beyond—comes alive in my hand.

There is nothing epic about what happens next. It's just me and the creek and the fish, but that is enough. The trout, a brown of 15 inches or thereabouts, glides easily into the net at last and it occurs to me that this is the first living creature that has lived up to my expectations in months. I cannot take my eyes away from the fish and its many colors. There are yellows and blacks and ambers lying there in the net with the creek water washing over them. There is even a bit of red on the sides; rich, perfect crimson, the color of a bleeding wound. I wet my hand and run my fingertips along the trout's sleek flanks, amazed at their absolute vitality.

Finally, I detach the tiny fly from the fish and peel the net away around it. The trout rights itself slowly, flicks its tail and disappears. I suppose that I could claim some elaborate form of moral credit for the beneficence of the release, but the decision has nothing to do with regard for life or ecological correctness or any of that.

I just don't have room in my life for a dead fish right now.

June 20. Golden Stones. Four browns.
Water temperature: 68 degrees.

I missed the hatch this morning. I tossed and turned half the night until I finally gave up, turned on the light, sat on the edge of my bed and slapped 10 milligrams of morphine into my thigh. *That ought to do it*, I remember thinking, and by God it did, because the next thing I knew, light was pouring in through the cabin door, announcing that I had somehow managed to survive another night.

Don't worry about the pharmacology. I am under strict medical supervision here. It's what they can do, they tell me. People in my circumstances are evidently expected to appreciate small favors. At any rate, there won't be any drug abuse in this cabin, give or take an occasional Scotch and water. The cabin belongs to my brother, John. At least it used to; John is dead now and it's not really clear to me who owns the place anymore. I just keep showing up every summer. Perhaps no one knows about my presence and perhaps no one cares. Either possibility is fine with me.

It is remarkable how little of my brother remains here. This was *his* cabin, after all. He found the place and fixed it up and let all of us come here to enjoy the fish and the peace and quiet, but now he seems to have vanished without a trace. You can't point to a single thing inside the cabin and say "Yeah, that was John." You would think there *would* be something, a photograph or an old shirt or some pleasantly bungled carpentry project, but the place feels barren of personality, so deliberately so that you wonder if he might have planned it that way.

Having dreamt away the morning and puttered away the afternoon, it is time to do the one important thing left for me to do, which is not to wallow in the memory of the dead (who can disappoint you every bit as much as the living), but to go fishing.

The creek is being capricious, however. There are no bugs hanging above its surface in the warm afternoon light. The trout are sleeping. I've got all the time in the world though, so I settle into the grass along the bank and study the water like a predator watching its unsuspecting prey.

Out in the current, a muskrat appears at the apex of a widening V and angles relentlessly toward the bank. Emerging from the water less than a rod length away, the animal looks like a sewer rat at first, but then it shakes its coat in the sun and its rich, lustrous fur fluffs up like a butterfly emerging from a cocoon. My mother—our mother—used to have a muskrat coat, back when I was little and John was even littler. I remember burying my face in those long, shaggy layers of maternal comfort, knowing, positively knowing, that everything was going to be all right. Now the living muskrat makes all that seem like yesterday, even though yesterday seems like a very long time ago indeed.

Finally my visitor disappears back into the water. The afternoon passes slowly. I am not in pain. It is the indifference of the stream in motion that I must come to terms with now. Gautama understood this, according to Buddhist legend. I can imagine him sitting on the riverbank and feel the intensity of his recognition that there is finally no upstream or downstream at all, but a continuous circular motion from heaven to earth to sea and back to heaven once again. Good for him. Of course, he never knew the exquisite perfection of a leveraged buyout, did he? He never slid his ass into the pilot's seat of a corporate jet and knew that the bloody thing was *his*. But that's his problem.

The Buddha didn't know everything. He probably didn't even know that he *had* a prostate, the treacherous gland that lurks deep in our male recesses, waiting to spew forth venom when we least expect it. That's one thing I understand that he didn't. Furthermore, he could not have been a fly fisherman, or else he never would have managed to hold still beside the stream long enough to surrender to that great emptiness inside. Just look at what is going on down on the water all of a sudden, where little yellow stoneflies are appearing, only to disappear once more in languid, sipping rises. The creek, so still for so long, is suddenly alive again, and that isn't the sort of thing people like me can sit through.

I rise to my feet and return to the water like an amphibian. The little yellow stones are one of the creek's sleeper hatches, but I've been here before, seen this, done that. There is a wad of perfect imitations buried in my vest, and as soon as I've got one tied to the tippet and out over the water at the head of the first pool, it is gone, consumed by a perfect dimple that leaves me fast to an equally perfect three-pound brown.

Who says religion is the opium of the masses?

**June 22. Pale Morning Duns. Sixteen rainbows, three browns.
Water temperature: 68 degrees.**

I spent the night listening to nighthawks buzz beneath the waning moon.

Everything is so quiet this morning; the cabin, the creek, the sky. I am very much alone. Ordinarily, this is anything but a problem, but every once in awhile, look out. There was a period of time just before dawn when I would have welcomed the company of anyone: ex-wives, IRS agents, bait fishermen, politicians. That passed quickly, but not quickly enough. Moods like that leave an unpleasant aftertaste, like wine stored behind a faulty cork. Let it linger and you'll gag on it all day long.

So up and at 'em, partner. Breakfast again. This egg's for you, Ma, but the whiskey in the coffee is just for me. Properly restored to a semblance of working order, I gather my things and head out the door toward the creek, which waits for me as eagerly as a steady girlfriend.

Not that I would know much about that. Overall, the women in my life have treated me about as well as my prostate. I'm sure I deserved a certain amount of treachery (from the women, that is), but still. Two wives, two daughters, two mistresses. And now they're all gone, vanished as certainly as my dead brother's shirts. Sometimes it's hard to remember their names. Trout streams never do that to you. Rivers don't betray people that way.

Down at the streamside, I settle into my waiting place along the bank and watch. Suddenly the surface is awash in delicate flecks of gold: *Ephemerella lacustris*, Pale Morning Duns.

Ephemerella! The name itself sounds like something out of a fairy tale; haunting, evocative, nothing you would associate with creatures as commonplace as bugs. Down on my knees at the very edge of the water, I watch the current carry its charges by in an endless invertebrate parade. Populated by things that bite and creep and build castles out of dung, the insect kingdom is a public relations nightmare, but this morning's mayflies are exquisite, like newly discovered relics from a vanished culture of artisans.

It is the operatic tempo of their lives as much as their physical beauty that separates the mayflies from the beetles and the chiggers and the wasps, however. The proud eruption taking place before me is only the prelude to despair, the few brief hours of license before the calamitous end.

If your eyes could follow the course of one dun among the many, you could sit right here and watch the whole thing: a life lived out in the air, complete with birthing and screwing and dying, a comic-book condensation of the things that fools like us take 60 years to do without ever managing to get it right.

Whatever dense metaphor the human imagination might make of *Ephemerella lacustris*, as far as the trout are concerned they are nothing more than entries on the menus. Now one rhythmic rise after another appears out in the slick along the edge of the fast current, until I can stand it no longer. I climb to my feet, check my tackle and press out into the stream. Water teases at my loins. Paired duns collide upon my shirt, copulating in fury. Then the first rainbow rises to my delicate imitation. Art is destroyed in the fish's mouth, but it doesn't matter. Finally, once again, I am *part* of something.

June 30.

Notice anything different? The smoke rising listlessly from the wood-stove is the product of no ordinary fuel. Decades of pointless field notes went up in flames last night. From barometer readings to body counts, they're all gone now. I came back to the cabin after fishing the spinner fall and realized what a joke they were. Those notes were the product of a positively aristocratic impulse. What we can't understand, we describe; what we can't describe, we tally. It's all ashes now.

Which is why there is no monotonous data at the beginning of this journal entry. *Of course* the water temperature is 68 degrees; this is a goddamn spring creek. *Of course* I caught some fish. There isn't anything else worthwhile to do out here, and whether I caught five fish or fifty isn't going to matter, not in the larger perspective.

I've spent most of my life being suspicious of people who looked at anything in the larger perspective. I had a marketing VP once, a bright kid, who walked into the boardroom one day and spent an hour talking about the failure of the corporate structure to address the larger perspective. I fired him. John used to go on like that too, right here in the cabin, until there wasn't anything to do but take off for the creek and hope the fish were biting. Now you heard it right here, from the old horse's mouth. What in God's name is happening?

I spent the day fishing. The names of the flies are not important. Neither is the number of fish caught, their species or their dimensions. That is why I didn't write any of it down. I am beyond scorekeeping. Why it took so long for this to happen is a mystery that leaves me awestruck.

It is early in the evening now. I have returned to the cabin to eat dinner. This is something of a figure of speech, as I have not really eaten dinner in months. The return to the table late in the day is mostly a matter of convention, a thing we do to reassure ourselves that we are social animals even when it should be clear that we are not. I have even taken the skillet down from the cupboard above the stove, placed something from the refrigerator inside it and let it warm. I have no intention of eating anything, but at least I am trying to be civil, to myself if no one else.

By the time this is done, the nighthawks are back, flapping gracefully through the summer air. The moon has darkened during the two weeks I have spent here. There is almost nothing left of it now as it floats like a ghost in the western sky, notable as much for the absence of light across its dark diameter as for the presence of light along its one remaining rim. I feel like the moon. I have come to terms with the fact that I am alone here, that I have always been alone, that I am doing something that we all must finally do in the company of no one but ourselves.

Beyond the porch, the creek rolls on. I can imagine the sound of trout rising in the darkness. It is possible that I have seen my last Pale Morning Dun. *Ephemerella*! People and mayflies have more in common than either might imagine. The differences in the scales of our lives are simply a matter of time, and that, as someone else has pointed out, is just something that the Swiss manufacture, the French squander, the Americans equate with money and the Hindus claim does not exist.

I remove the fly rod from its resting place on the porch and start down the steps toward the sound of the creek. The air is gravid with the smell of flowers. Pain climbs up my spine, but there is no need to worry about that any more.

I am not going gently into the night. I am going fishing.

ghost pain

Harry Humes

My father had one arm. Coal scars on his face blue as deep water, and he was a fly fisherman, maybe the best in our part of the coal region. Before the gas explosion in his mine, he made fine wood rods. There were always culms of bamboo hanging from the ceiling in the back cellar. After a supper of potato soup and black tea, he used to go down to the cellar, taking up his knife and mallet and splitting the long pieces of bamboo and then splitting them again, rubbing his fingers over them, looking for knots or flaws in the grain, scuffs or scars. Any errant behavior in the wood, as he put it. All winter down there in his heavy sweater, straightening the strips over a flame, planing and tapering, gluing and wrapping. One morning there it would be on the kitchen table, six coats of varnish, red silk wraps, guides and ferrules shining. When he'd put one in my hands, it'd tremble through the cork handle and want to fly off. He'd test-cast them in the garden, his arm hardly moving, the new rod bending behind him then arcing forward, line unwinding from the narrow loop over his head, almost invisible against the sky. He told me that bamboo was a grass and that the first bamboo rod makers also made violins.

After the accident, after the long hospital stay and after almost a year during which our house seemed to grow smaller and smaller, filled with pockets of silence and pain, my father one evening began trying to tie a clinch knot. He held the leader in his teeth or under the stump of his left arm, the leader slipping, the whole thing unraveling, my father cursing, throwing it all to the floor and walking out. Another day, he took out his favorite rod from its tube and fit the three sections together. It reached the length of our living room in that narrow row house. The tip grazed Aunt Maude's photograph on the piano and almost tipped over one of my mother's cups from Nova Scotia.

It was snowing, wind blowing fiercely up Ash Alley, the coal train's wheels slipping on the rails, but there my father was, the long wood rod in his hands, smiling, telling me April to come we'd be out again on the Big Pine or Loyalsok or Penn's. "Just let me get the hang of this one-armed business," he said, bouncing the rod gently off my red hair.

When my mother came home from her Dorcas Society or Eastern Star meeting, she stamped some life back into her feet, saying, "Well, it's a fine place to be fishing, right in the middle of my living room."

"How are the ladies?" my father asked. "All stiff and conceited with Bible verses?"

My mother smiled. "Just go on with your old rods and leave the ladies to me."

Eventually, my father managed two or three knots, and when the weather warmed up, he went into our backyard to practice his casting. He kept a short line and mostly rolled it out to one spot, then to another, intent as ever, as if trout were feeding under the stalks of last summer's peonies or sage.

In April, off we went in the DeSoto, my father driving out of our valley along the blacktop road below Packer Five, all black and smoking away up there on its plateau, the big car leaving behind the spill banks and dirty water, and then suddenly out of it, and the landscape changing to Brush Valley, the long, narrow reservoir and miles of fields and clear water, not the orange acid water of the streams back home.

In the pre-dawn dark, the miles slipped by. My father shifted with his right arm, holding the steering wheel with his knees, occasionally asking me to pour him a little coffee from the thermos. When he took a sip, he asked, "Are you really going to use that fancy new outfit?"

I nodded. "I can get farther out with it. And you need hardly any weight."

"What's it called?"

"A spinning outfit. A whole new way of fishing. The spool doesn't move. The line peels off it. It's nifty."

My father smiled at me but said nothing. I wanted to tell him how I'd gone up by the railroad tracks above our house to practice, using one of my mother's clothespins for weight. I got so I could drop it by the switch or right next to a pile of ties. As the passenger trains rumbled by to Pottsville or Williamsport, white faces looking out, I imagined swirls of water behind rocks and the silver sides of trout and their black backs, the feel of them at the end of my line. And something else, too, that I could never put into words.

A thin line of red hung just above the hills when we stopped for gas. There was a small fishing shop at the back of the store—vests, a few rods, reels, leaders, three big plastic boxes, their compartments brim-full of flies, all of them the color of early spring, all of them poised as if to fly or swim off. My father picked one out. "Here's the one for today," he said, turning it softly to the light. Then still holding the caddis up in front of him, he turned to me. "Did you bring the other rod just in case?"

In one corner of the store, a potbellied stove glowed, its chrome front shining, a curved handle stuck in the plate on top. A kettle of water steamed away. The chimney went up on an angle to the ceiling, then bent quickly and out through the wall. In the coal scuttle next to the stove, a tin shovel, a candy bar wrapper, a few feathers.

"Ah, Reed, you left it home, didn't you? I remember seeing it in the corner before we left. That's a shame, for they'll be all over the water today. Wait and see. You should have brought it along." A piece of coal popped and splintered against the window of the stove.

Then moving again, the road following the stream, rising and falling, the car swaying around bends, and here and there an occasional fisherman pulling on his boots, smoking, waving as we passed, and my father humming, slowing for the bad bump before the bridge, then turning onto the dirt road.

"Looks like no one's been in yet. We'll have it to ourselves."

Buck laurel scraped along the windows and fenders, the DeSoto's fluid-drive transmission clanked and whirred into lower gears and then we slowed to a stop. All of it the same, as if winter had never happened, as if my father still had two arms. The fir trees on the far side hung out over the water, and behind them the land rose steeply, pausing at a narrow shelf before climbing again toward the ridge. It all seemed to flow out of the stream.

My father let out his breath. "Glory be," he said. "This is what I think about every day. A far cry from that old water back home, eh? What do you say, old Reed, old boy?" He put his right hand on my shoulder and rubbed it in small circles. Even with one arm, he was never more in balance than when he was near trout water. His whole being changed, his face surfacing, as if from one of his tunnels, swimming up.

"Well, what are we waiting for? Can't you hear them out there calling to us, telling us to get a move on, that they'll not stick around all morning?"

My father had a routine from the moment he opened the trunk. First the tube with the rod inside, then his worn vest with its pockets stuffed with leaders, fly boxes, scissors, a small container of split-shot in case he was forced to drag a nymph along the bottom of the stream. He'd place the vest on the ground next to the rod tube, telling me for the thousandth time not to step on them, please, and next getting into his waders, old and patched, still leaking in places he'd not found or could not fix. All of it so familiar, the faded red suspenders over the shoulders of the pea coat. Once in a while he'd grind his head into his left shoulder and groan softly, his lips a straight line.

It was the ghost pains, he once told me. It was his body thinking the arm was still there instead of a half-mile underground. He reached down for his vest. "Well, how do I look?" he asked when he was all fitted out. "Ready for the ball?"

Last, he stuck the tube under his stump and unscrewed the top with his hand, a slight scratching of threads as he did, holding the cap in his mouth as he pulled out the bag with the rod inside. It was the way he moved through all of it that I loved, turning the pieces in his hand, putting aside the extra tip, fitting the middle section in place, then the last, lining up the guides, holding it out into the morning. When he moved his hand slightly, the rod moved as if it were alive.

He looked at my shorter, stiffer rod, the sleek reel with its 100 yards of four-pound-test monofilament. I turned away toward the water.

"You go ahead," he said. "I'll just fish up here and be along. Go on. They're calling you."

"Let me put the reel on and run the line through for you," I said. He shooed me off, saying he'd have a cup of coffee and think about things a little, then he'd be along.

The water was cold from snow melt and running high and swift along the side of the rock we called Moody's Rock for the man who used to fish from it. Two mergansers flew over, and a mink slithered across some scree and vanished behind a windfall.

My father was right. The fish were calling, nice chunky browns that slashed at my lure, the short rod bent over, the line disappearing into the water.

My father finally came down to the stream, his rod trailing behind him like a narrow wake. When he saw me he tucked it under his stump and waved, then signaled he was going downstream. I was hoping he'd use that hand gesture of his to ask if I'd had any luck.

I turned away, reaching farther and farther out across the pool, my lure sometimes skittering impatiently up out of the water, sometimes catching on bottom rocks. We were still the only fishermen on this part of the stream. I could cast in any direction, send my line arcing far out, clicking the bail shut, then retrieving it, the click and whir of the gears, casting again and again, covering the pool top to bottom, impatient to tell my father about this new way of fishing, how easy it was, how far out I could reach.

And I did tell him, on our way home, doing a dumb show there in the car, casting out, reeling in with my left hand, making my strike, fighting the fish.

My father smiled. "Sounds pretty good," he said. "Maybe I should try it."

And then something swept over me, exploded in my heart, took part of the day away. I remembered the way my father used to come up the steps from that back cellar, his face easy and unscarred, telling us how much he'd got done on the new rod, rubbing his hands, asking my mother if there was any tea left. He gave a name to each rod he made—The Old Philosopher, The Mammoth, Evening Sun, Rescue the Perishing—and kept a list describing each of them in one of his mining notebooks.

And then I remembered watching him earlier that day, after I'd cleaned my limit and had them in my creel under wet grass and leaves. He had been sitting on a rock along the stream when I came down the trail, pushing his head again into his left shoulder, trying to chase away the pain. Even from where I was I could hear him grunting and moaning. I stopped and stood watching; after a while he got up and began stripping a little line off the small English reel, his long bamboo rod darting forward and the line rolling over itself above the water, as if it were making its way to some secret place. He'd slip on a rock, catch his balance, move on, a man all by himself, intently working the water, reading its rhythms, striking every so often against a trout, his rod graceful, a kind of lyrical presence in the morning. He'd work a trout slowly, steadily, not wanting to exhaust it or damage it, and when he had it in, he'd stick the rod under his stump and slide his right hand down the line and slip the fish off the barbless hook. Then he'd stand there, staring at the water where the fish had vanished, or lift his head up and around, nodding at the hills and ridges. Just standing there as if he were in church with me and my mother, just before the hymn began. And then my father would start up again, making his slow way along the edge, fishing close, water pushing and splashing against his legs, casting and casting, the line rolling gracefully out, as if he were writing something on the water in a language it would take me years to learn to read and understand.

uncle sergei's madness

Joel Parkman

My mother told me that Uncle Sergei was working in the plants at Chelyabinsk No. 65 when the accident took place in year 1957. It was much worse than Chernobyl but of course things were very secret then. First of all you must know that my Uncle Sergei is not a drunk. He drinks vodka like the rest of us in Russia, to stay warm when it is cold and when it is not cold we drink because it will surely be cold again. So this thing is a madness you see, not drunkenness.

My mother blames the big explosion in the nuclear plant, the one in year 1957, for Uncle Sergei's madness. But she has always blamed all the world's troubles on that day. In year 1986 when there was no more sausage in the whole town, she said it was because of the accident and when there was no soap it was the same thing. Now there is sausage and soap and she blames the high prices on the accident. Maybe nuclear radiation can cause inflation, I don't know personally but I have not heard this theory from the experts, only from my mother.

Many of my uncle's friends come to him to visit. He once made the long trip to Moscow to receive the Order of Lenin for his work at the plant. Many said that it was his work that made the plant safe again and I have heard in whispers that he was as brilliant as Sakharov but only born too late to invent the bombs that made the Soviet Union a superpower. My mother said if he had not been so proud and ambitious he would have gone to Moscow to teach at the institute there instead of showing off until they couldn't run the plant without him. But he stayed and was there when it blew up. They say his hair fell out then. I personally have seen a picture of him as a young man, shaking Khrushchev's hand with a head of thick dark hair and this is after 1957. But in the picture of him with Brezhnev he is as bald as Khrushchev was in the earlier picture.

So I must tell you about my uncle's madness. It did not come to him until the time of Gorbachev or perhaps it was Yeltsin already, I am not exactly sure. But I know it began when the Americans came, though my mother says it comes from year 1957. The Americans came here to make a deal with the Uralneftegaz. One of those joint ventures where the Americans give money to the Russian oil company and the mafia gets rich. But that is another madness.

One American was a geologist and he came to talk to the experts and to look at the maps and the geophysical studies carried out by scientists from the Oil and Gas Institute named for Gubkin. My uncle was invited to meet him as one of the important citizens in our city. Soon the experts and my uncle and the other important citizens were all drinking vodka with this American scientist. I was there, you see, as a translator so I hear every word, spoke most of them as well, I must say. The American was a big man who liked to laugh and talk and to drink vodka. His company was the Montana Oil and Gas Company.

But this scientist, he didn't want to talk about oil and gas or about American dollars. He wanted to talk about Montana. You see I bring my story to this point because I believe, whatever my mother says about year 1957, this is the very moment when my uncle Sergei's madness began.

Mr. Dobbs, this is the big man, the scientist, he began to say that in the spring that the insects begin to hatch and fly about above the water of the rivers. He said that the water was so clean that a man could see its bottom and that the fish lived there still in great numbers. The fishes are so thick they will eat your flies from your pocket if you wade into the water, he told us. My uncle took another drink of vodka. I saw him at this moment do this when he stared into the eyes of the great American scientist. (You see he told us he had studied at the great University of Tulsa.) So my uncle listens to Mr. Dobbs tell about this thing called fishing flies. No, not flies like the ones in the market or at the hospital. But insects, especially ones that fly. Mr. Dobbs took one of the papers from his briefcase and with a special red knife from Switzerland, I could see the Swiss cross on the side, you see, he took out a staple that held the papers together. This tiny piece of wire he bent into the shape of a hook and then cut a tiny thread from his coat. My uncle watched this very closely. Then the American tied the thread around the staple and snipped bits and pieces of the thread with a tiny pair of scissors from his red knife from Switzerland. We were all amazed that the tiny staple looked so much like an insect it was as if it would fly away!

Mr. Dobbs said that fishing rods that were long and thin would be used to cast a thick floating line upon which was tied a tiny invisible line called a great leader. I remember this term because all of the old men laughed and drank a toast to any great leader that was invisible. Then the fish would be fooled by the hook that looked like an insect and be captivated.

"Couldn't you captivate a fish with a worm like my grandfather did down at the river?" Uncle asked. Mr. Dobbs was shocked, this is considered crude, and you must understand that this is when my uncle's madness began, I remember his eyes, it was at this exact moment. Mr. Dobbs the great American scientist told my father that fishing flies was not a sport for the killing of fish but a great and noble art and a science and that its meaning was found in the exact replication of nature. A true fisherman of flies did not kill and eat his captivated fish but sent them back to live in the river.

At this point Mr. Dobbs began a long speech. He rose to make a toast, for he had seen how we Russians rose and gave great toasts by which we entertain ourselves on cold winter nights. This speech he gave about the beauty of nature, which he called his mother and the big heaven of Montana, which he said was known to everyone as Big Heaven Country. They even write it on their automobiles. A great tear came to his eye when he spoke and everyone knew that he was a man with a great soul.

"God almighty," he said. "It's fine country."

There was a long pause in my translation because I had never heard this phrase, "God almighty" before. For a long time I thought hard and then remembered an old book my grandmother had written in. It was always behind the *Works of Lenin,* out of sight, but like every child, I found all the secret places. So I translated this phrase, "God almighty."

The men looked frightened at first. Then they looked for a long time at the American who was standing quietly and appearing at peace at the evocation of Montana and God.

One by one the men stood up and raised their glasses. "God almighty," each said with great, how do you say in English?, solemnness. Later Uncle told me he had only heard this phrase from his own grandmother when he was a little boy. He was sure each of those old men with us that night had heard from their grandmothers in their childhoods and almost surely not since. He believed because of this phrase that Mr. Dobbs was a prophet, though, I must say, he never said this to me personally.

It was these solemn words that began my uncle's madness. For Mr. Dobbs—he was a great soul, a deep man and his love of nature that he called his mother—moved my uncle and at this moment he was converted to this love and the Great Heaven of Montana. I think this was his madness.

That night when there was no more black bread and the smoked salmon was gone, when there were no more pickles and there were only a few bottles of vodka and of Pepsi-Cola, my uncle, Mr. Dobbs and I sat up and talked about fishing flies. Mr. Dobbs talked about the exact scientific facts about the insects upon which the American fishes called trout, rainbows, cuts, and brownies fed. We were amazed that he spoke of these insects in Latin and we knew he was a great scientist indeed if he was both a geologist and a specialist in the biological sciences.

There was not much vodka left when Mr. Dobbs spoke of the fine art of throwing a fly with the exact way by which a skilled fisherman could captivate one of those river fishes, which must be far more intelligent than normal fishes. I believe that this is from the great natural selection where only the strongest live to reproduce and those fishes not intelligent enough to evade captivity were destroyed and only the stronger would carry forward the history. But I am not sure because now a new truth about the history is true. Mr. Dobbs stood and held his pen like a fishing fly rod and acted out the proper means of making a throw. He demonstrated the classic throw and something he called a roll throw. His right hand went up and down as if it had a rod in it. His left hand remained below his waist and moved up and down also, or out from his side, but my uncle and I did not understand this motion.

When the American company quarreled with the General Director of Uralneftegaz and there was no contract and no joint venture, the Americans went away. My uncle was saddened to see the scientist and prophet Mr. Dobbs go and for many days he would walk down to the river and watch the dead water flow by. There had not been fish there for many years. My mother said not since year 1957. Soon he was looking at maps and tracing the routes of Russia's great rivers with his fingertips and marking the places where he knew the plants were. The Volga, the Don, the Ob and many others. He began going on the weekends out to the country looking at the local rivers. "Just to see," he said. My mother was angry because he was not helping with the summer garden at our dacha. But still he went looking for rivers of clean water.

Soon he was discussing in whispers around our kitchen table until late at night a secret project with many of his old engineering friends. They argued and laughed but whispered when they bent over their drawings. After these many secret meetings he began to not come home at night and on the weekends he would go to the machine shop at the plant. He was very excited and nervous at this time. Then one day he came home with his first fly rod. It was made from high-grade aluminum and was about as thick at its base as my last finger and then got very thin. It was about four meters long and there was not room in our flat big enough to keep it without it jutting across the room. For many weeks he made loops on the rod for the line and then he put on it one of the reels that the fishermen once used when they fished through the ice. This is not done anymore because the plant will sometimes expel much hot water suddenly into the river. So the ice will melt and the old men fishing always will fall through the ice and are not found again until springtime far down the river.

Uncle Sergei stayed up many nights all the night through making a line for his rod. The line used by all the old ice fishermen would not float in the bathtub, even if it was rubbed with wax. So Uncle Sergei tried many materials before deciding that silk fibers could be woven together to make a very light line that would float if it were properly waxed. He traded some of the materials from the plant to an old comrade from Korea who sent him much fine silk. He was able to weave it into a short line and then get some of the old babushkas to make him many meters of line for his reel.

Uncle Sergei had an aluminum rod, silk line for his rod, some of the old fishing line that was small enough for an invisible leader and a reel. By this time the winter was ending and Uncle Sergei's attention turned to the biological sciences. Our kitchen-table engineers were replaced by specialists from the biological institute and books were found on the nature and behavior of the insects in Russia. Uncle Sergei went away every weekend during this summer to collect insects, again hearing my mother's complaints about tending the dacha garden without him. These insects he stuck with little pins onto boards with their names in Latin. He was very proud of his collection and was soon as much an expert as the biologists from the institute and even wrote some papers for their thick scientific journals on the insects that lived along Russia's rivers.

He had kept Mr. Dobbs' staple tied when the American first taught Uncle Sergei about fishing flies. When he could not collect insects he was collecting materials for his next round of experiments. He obtained from the old ice fishermen some hooks and had the machine shop at the plant make him some very tiny hooks from the special materials they had there. He was especially proud of those made from boron and titanium. Every visitor was inspected and samples were collected from their hair and from the collars of their coats so that Uncle could test them in the manufacture of these flies. He went to the markets and even took the trains into Siberia to collect furs and feathers and fabrics to try his skills at imitating the insects he collected. He had studied the habits of the fishes that live in rivers with his friends at the institute and classified his efforts into several areas. Foremost was the *Ephemerella*. It was a fly that lived in several stages and Uncle Sergei had a very sophisticated scientific theory that in order to captivate the intelligent fishes, he must use the exact imitation of the exact form of the insect in its exact stage that the fishes were eating at that exact moment. He called his theory "the exact representation of the concurrent stage of metamorphosis of insects in the habitat of the feeding river fishes." Night after night he experimented making his boron and titanium hooks look like the insects. He stopped smoking because he did not want his fingers to smell when he tied each exact representation. He stopped drinking vodka so that his hands would be steady when he tied the badger fur with threads from Bulgarian suits. This is when it became apparent to people beyond our own family that Uncle Sergei had gone mad.

Another sign of madness was that Uncle welcomed the coming of the winter. He had put his silk line in the river only once as a test and the sample had almost disintegrated in the harsh water. So he never again tested his equipment in the waters of the Urals. Instead he waited for the clean snow to cover Chelyabinsk No. 65. When the first snow was on the ground he took his aluminum rod, attached the reel, placed some of the babushka-woven silk line on the reel and went out into the courtyard of our building to make his first throws. This was the first time I saw my uncle drink vodka since his madness had made him manufacture flies. His aluminum rod was a failure. I watched as his line flopped back and forth but would not fly from him. His rod was stiff and his line went over his head and back, pounding on the snow in front of him exactly where he had laid it out first with his hands. I could tell he was angry, but as a scientist he took up his line, walked with his rod back up to the flat and began again with his drawings.

The engineers returned to our flat and late-night planning sessions took place. Only Uncle Sergei refraining from the vodka. They discussed many materials and prototypes were built simultaneously to be tested. Rods were made of different lengths and thicknesses from boron and titanium by the same shops that made Uncle's hooks and reactor cores. Variations were produced also of the aluminum, which may simply have been a failure of design, not materials. Craftsmen were recruited to fashion prototypes from different woods. Uncle noticed bamboo baskets from the East in the marketplace and again materials were shipped to Korea in exchange for more silk and a shipment of bamboo. All winter Uncle was in the courtyard, testing rods on the snow. He tested each rod carefully using a variety of experimental techniques for the throw. Physicists from the plant and from the institute of physical and theoretical sciences now occupied the kitchen tables and the aerodynamic patterns of silk lines were studied and predicted under different circumstances. He experimented, very carefully recording each variation of design, materials, and methods.

By the time the winter had grown old, Uncle had decided the best of all the rods was one made from the bamboo. Approximately three meters long, it was made not from a single long bamboo but from six straight pieces split and glued together to make a thin rod of a stiffness appropriate to the properties of the silk line. He was very proud of this rod, especially when he discovered that the line would fly forward best when a proper method of throwing was employed. He was careful to not bring his rod too far back and he taught the babushkas to weave a line that began thin and thickened for several meters, giving it more weight, and then thinning again so it could be pulled behind when the thicker portion was thrown forward. All of the engineers, physicists and even the biologists were impressed with the technical achievement.

But he was unable to test his theory of the exact representation of the concurrent stage of metamorphosis of insects in the habitat of the feeding river fishes. When the spring came and the time of the insect hatching came, Uncle was unable to find water that had fish in it. Week after week he went to the country but could not find moving water in which the trout could live. Surely, up in the Urals there were streams of high, cold, moving water, swarming with *Ephemerella* being eaten in their concurrent stages of metamorphosis by hungry fishes. But if there were, he could not get to them from Chelyabinsk No. 65. The maps that were available were deliberately inaccurate; Chelyabinsk No. 65 was not even on them. They were designed to protect the motherland, not to guide an expert in atomic physics and biological sciences to a moving stream of innocent water. Whenever he would follow the maps to a promising valley it would either not exist or be dead from the byproduct of his own plant or from Soviet experiments.

Soon the short summer was over and winter began to return. Uncle, who had persevered through war, hardship and purge, sat defeated among his prototype rods, his bags full of animal fur and feathers and reel after reel of silk line and invisible leaders. When the first snow fell I saw my uncle weep.

My mother said that he was mad and that it was all because of year 1957. She said that of course all the fish were dead and that also was the fault of year 1957 and in this she may have been right. "Your mother the nature is just an old tired babushka like us all," she said, as bitter as Uncle was sad.

For weeks Uncle went on as dead. He went to the plant, he came home. The television showed smiling women selling pet food and young happy Americans selling Coca-Cola. Uncle just stared out of the window past the television at the falling snow. It was worse one evening, very late when Uncle went to buy cigarettes from a kiosk. He didn't care anymore if his fingers stank. I went with him, just to get out from the flat. We came to a kiosk that was full of the usual candy bars, juice and a hundred bottles of sweet alcohol and vodka, rock-and-roll cassettes and videotapes. Uncle looked and there was a carton of cigarettes called "Montana." He stared a long time at the carton. He bought the cigarettes and on the way home he took all of the packs from it and stuffed them into my pockets. He held the white carton with the word "Montana" written on it in big red letters.

"I want to go to the Big Heaven Country," he said. "I will go there where the fishes are so thick they will eat flies from your pocket if you wade into the water." I remember that Mr. Dobbs said this, about the fishes eating flies from his pockets.

The next day Uncle went and applied for his foreign passport. He paid 300 American dollars to the man in the office there to make sure he got his papers. He made the long trip to Moscow to apply for a visa from the American embassy.

After long weeks of waiting, the visa from the Americans came. "Approved" said the forms in both Russian and English. Uncle began to plan his trip and he obtained a map of America and carefully studied the rivers in the state of Montana. He packed his flies tied on the hooks of boron and titanium. He cut his best bamboo rods in half and fitted them with joints so he could carry them with him on the airplane and they would not be stolen by the Aeroflot ground crews.

Uncle laughed and drank again around the kitchen table with his friends that winter. He cursed the government and the mafia and they talked about how great the old days were, even when there was great hardship, just like they had always done. He planned his trip for the late winter, believing it would be spring already in the Big Heaven Country.

One morning Uncle did not wake up. The doctors said it was probably a heart attack. They did not have the time to be sure. Two weeks after Uncle died, a letter came from the Ministry of Foreign Affairs informing Uncle Sergei in bureaucratic language that as one who knew important state secrets he could not be allowed to travel overseas. He was encouraged to continue in his patriotic work on behalf of Russia and that after a period of five years he would be eligible to apply again for a foreign passport.

I have thought about my Uncle Sergei since that time of his madness. I do not believe it is the fault of year 1957. I also believe that in all the time it was not the madness of captivating the clever fishes by using the theory of the exact representation of the concurrent stage of metamorphosis of insects in the habitat of the feeding river fishes. I believe it was the hope of the Big Heaven Country. He had hoped he could find the Big Heaven in Russia and then in Montana, America. Maybe that hope was madness. My country has hoped in Big Heaven before. I do not know what the experts say about this. But I think that maybe now Uncle has found the Big Heaven Country and I hope that he is representing the concurrent stages of those insects there and captivating the fishes.

for keeps

Gary Whitehead

After the rain we walk a blue road, the overhanging trees watching themselves drip. Two blackbirds on a post-and-rail fence drink from their red wings. When Rich stops to light his pipe, I stop too, slide my eight-footer from its case, pull out my old Pflueger and seat it. Barely audible, almost a trick of the ears, the river beyond the willows sings the spring thaw, the added rain. Mountains to the east, mountains to the west, and between both ranges this famous river that has gurgled through my dreams since I was a boy. I feed the line through the guides and tie on a Blue-Wing Olive. Rich is so excited he's shaking and laughing, tobacco strips spilling out of his charred pipe.

"Hold on," he says, "let me get my camera, Larold. Let me get the Polaroid." When he's ready, I check for clearance, fix on a puddle in the road, flex the rod like shaking a flame from it and cast into the blue reflection of sky. The camera clicks and whirs.

Rich says, "Larold, you . . . I . . . you never caught no fish here." A long string of saliva swings from his beard. Apple smoke trails out of his nose, making him look like a dragon. Even with his stained teeth, his untrimmed beard, his uneven eyes—the left one blind as eternity—he's still a handsome man, like our father was.

"Wait till we get to the river," I say, grinning. "Save your film for the trout." But the camera shoots out another black square of film, and Rich waves it in the air, dancing while the picture paints itself.

"For keeps," he says, offering it to me. When he's done laughing, he puffs on the old stained pipe like a kid drinking juice through a straw.

The Battenkill. River of legend, river of Orvis, river that pulsed in the ears of Ethan Allen and his Green Mountain Boys as they defended against the redcoats. Here it riffles frothily around a bend, evens out in a pool as dark as cola. Swords of sun slash through willows dripping light. There's a sandy ramp down to the water, only a quarter-mile from the B&B where we've just checked in, a house that once belonged to Ira Allen, Ethan's brother. It's no wonder the British wanted this country. No wonder our great-grandfathers' great-grandfathers took it from those who were here first, then fought to keep it. Old guilt wrapped up in old pride, and I still can't believe that Dad sold the cabin.

"This spot looks good as any," I say to Rich, who's canting his head, looking cautious. He peers at the river from 10 feet away, his good eye flashing, his murky eye as steady and dead as what gazes up out of a creel. When he was a boy he loved the water. Summers when we came to the cabin, before Dad sold it, Rich would swim and wade all day if we let him. Now he's afraid of water, will only shower when Gerry or I beg him to. Something he picked up from the two years he spent at the "special" school. Like eating with his arm wrapped around his plate, one hand over his glass. The worst two years of my life, and I can't imagine what they must have been for him. After he sent Rich off, I could hardly look at Dad, never mind speak to him. Even after he grew a heart and fetched Rich back, I still wouldn't trust him. I remember them walking in the house, Rich 14 and gangly under Dad's arm, the two of them smiling as if he were only coming home from summer camp. What else could Rich do but love Dad more for letting him come home? He didn't know any better. Or maybe he did. Maybe I've just never been good at forgiving. One thing for sure, Rich no longer liked water. So I know now before I say it what his answer will be, but I say anyway, "I've got an extra set of waders if you want to join me."

"Larold, I'll wait . . . I . . . you go ahead. I'm gonna have a smoke." He sits on a fat root beneath one of the willows and packs his pipe, a ritual that keeps him even. I don't complain about it the way Gerry does. She says it's dangerous and that I don't know because I'm no longer there. She says Rich smokes in bed and that he pulls the batteries out of the three smoke alarms upstairs because he doesn't like the noise they make. She puts the batteries back, he pulls them out again. I've talked to him about smoking in bed, but how do you tell a grown man he can't enjoy a smoke in his own room? Whenever I visit them in Jersey now, Gerry brings it up, rides him about it. But if the old myth about stepmothers is true, Gerry's the exception. She's done more for Rich than anyone. And when I'm not visiting, she's all Rich has besides his friends at the workshop.

"Larold, old Gerry, she don't have no car," he says, as if reading my mind.

"Nope." She don't.

"How come, Larold, how come?"

"Dad tried to teach her once, but she didn't catch on." And hell, he was a driving instructor! I remember his taking Gerry out in the drivers-ed car the year before I moved to Iowa. It was a Ford specially equipped with a steering wheel and pedals on both sides. With Gerry in the driver's seat, Dad pointed out the pedals and the gear shift, what he called the "prindle." It was a lecture he'd given a thousand times, same one he'd given to me when I was 15: "Hands at ten and two, not at six! Easy on the brake! Watch your blind spots!" Gerry nodded at his every word. But when Dad started the car, she said, "Take me into town. I need a loaf of bread." After that, whenever he drove her anywhere he operated the car from the passenger's seat, out of spite.

"She probably couldn't hack it," Rich says.

And I can see where this is going. "I guess not."

"I got my license 10 years . . . 20 years ago. Didn't I Larold?"

"Heck, then you should have driven us up here," I say, stepping into my waders. It's true, he has a license, though it's long since expired. Dad helped him get it. Persuaded the state to give Rich an oral test because he couldn't read. Of course, Rich never drove. He just liked knowing that he could if he wanted to. I think what he likes most is the document itself. He's fascinated by anything official—badges, stamps, coins, diplomas. Gerry says he's collecting sweepstakes junk mail now. He's even asked about framing one of the letters.

He reaches into his pocket, takes out the worn license, holds it up for me to see. So I tease, "Maybe I'll let you drive Monday on the ride back down to Jersey."

He puffs on his pipe, squints his one good eye. "Larold, I like to walk. Never mind now, never mind."

That he's always called me Larold makes complete sense. My name's actually Lawrence, but I go by Larry. Since Harry's short for Harold, it follows that Larry must be short for Larold, at least in Rich's way of thinking. When he first started calling me Larold, when we were kids, we all tried to correct him, then gave up. How can you argue with that kind of logic?

Rich is anomalous, my word for developmentally disabled, or what the more insensitive call retarded. A problem of birth—fetal anoxia—or so the doctors said. Whatever the case, it never mattered to me. He was my little brother, the kid in the bottom bunk who'd talk me to sleep with his questions. My shadow. My brother. I bloodied many a lip in the schoolyards and playgrounds making damned sure everyone knew it, too. Hard to believe he turns 32 tomorrow. He looks little more than half that old. His thick, straight hair and beard are as light as shellacked bamboo. My head, on the other hand, is balding and going gray, and I'm only a year his senior. The ante a body pays for its better-dealt hand?

"Go on now, catch a fish. Go on Larold," Rich says.

I zip up my vest, clip the hemostat to the pocket and wink. "What do you want first, a brookie or a rainbow?"

"A rainbow," he says, "I like a rainbow."

I love the feel of wading into running water, the cool and complete hug it gives, the urgency with which the water curves and curls against the obstacle you make for it. I imagine something living slipping between my legs, the pace of a glacier's wisdom quickened by the change from solid to liquid. The hatch and spawn—of something as small as a fly or as grand as a civilization—that a river inspires. I love the extension that the rod makes of the arm, that the line makes of the rod, that the leader makes as it fades invisibly toward the tippet—a longer reach toward whatever greater thing moves all of us.

When I cast, I turn my head to watch the line arc behind me, fly above me, and I think of the barn swallows of Iowa, the longest days of summer playing out over a landscape I came to love as much as any mountain. Four years there, watching the tenancy of seasons, learning as much from the land as I did from any professor. The lesson of the hip-high pastures I'd wade through to watch deer at the salt lick. Pastures that, once mown, the tractors would lump into bales like great wheels. And out of the black bowls of their shadows the swallows pivoting, downing white moths out of the dusty air.

So I try to mimic the grace of those purple birds as I shoot line to reach the splashy rises upstream. The wing of my arm becoming the wing of the bird, which becomes the wing of the fly, all for the rising trout, whose wings happen to be fins, whose flyway happens to be water. How can you not believe in evolution?

More splashy rises now. A caddis hatch, or so I'm hoping. The rings are far upstream, there's flotsam in the water from the rain, lots of small bits of leaf and wood, and so it's tough to tell. "Catch a sample to be sure," Dad says in my head, sounding like a guidebook.

The last time I saw him alive was in August up in Narragansett, almost a year ago. I'd been in the new place long enough to empty the moving boxes and mow the lawn before I invited everybody up for a clambake, a weekend at the beach. They'd missed my graduation, but I didn't blame them, Iowa being halfway across the country. Besides, they'd already seen me graduate twice. This was our small reunion.

"Do we have to call you doctor now?" was the first thing Dad said.

Gerry looked harried from the drive. "Next time, you come to New Jersey. We'll take you to a real Jersey diner."

Rich squeezed hardest. "Been a long . . . too long . . . long time no see," he said. His hair was washed. His neck shaved. I could smell the Old Spice he borrowed from Dad.

I showed them around the house, then around the town swarming with summer tourists. In the evening, I dug a pit in the backyard for a traditional Rhode Island clambake. Codfish wrapped in cheesecloth, aluminum foil and seaweed, all cooked over wood coals. Steamed littlenecks, stuffed quahogs. Later that night we fished from the pier, casting jigs for blues, Rich taking pictures of the sailboats with his Polaroid through his one good eye. And I like to remember Dad this way, even though neither one of us cared a whole hell of a lot for saltwater fishing, or the ocean for that matter: I like to remember him and me at the end of a wooden dock, casting for blues, the foghorn honking its warning into the vast shroud of fog.

"Wake up," I say, shaking his boot, and Rich struggles to his feet. "It's going to rain again. We should get back." The sun gone, the sky is completely overcast, going dark in the west. Now and again there's a low rumbling out of the south.

Rich blinks, sweeps the dead grass from his khakis. "Larold, you catch anything, Larold?"

"Two browns. But they were small, too small for keeps."

He holds up the camera. "I wanted to take pictures of them, Larold."

"I know, but I didn't want to wake you, and I'd waded pretty far out. Hear the thunder? It's going to rain again."

"I'm hungry."

"For a minute there I thought that thunder was your stomach."

"Larold, I fell asleep . . . how was it . . . were they biting? Were they biting, Larold?"

"Not as much as we'll be. Come on, let's go get cleaned up, then we'll drive up to Manchester for spaghetti."

It's amazing how the capitalism this country was built on works to ruin it. Where there should be woods and rivers, maybe a road or two and some homes, there are strip malls, outlet stores, hotels, a Ben & Jerry's, a McDonald's, a Mexican cantina. I steer the truck through the early season traffic, wishing I'd caught keepers. I could've cleaned them at the river, asked Judy at the B&B to cook them up for us simple, sautéed with butter, string beans on the side.

We could've eaten them in Ethan Allen's brother's house, listening to old music in a room older than this country's independence. I think of Ethan writing his petition for statehood, writing by candlelight late into the night, his head heavy as a cannonball, while the beloved woods around him fill with neon lights, yellow arches.

Still, the town is charming in spite of the commercialism. In the light drizzle, people amble under umbrellas along the strip, past the windows of the old, invitingly lit Victorian homes, the small birches along the walkways twinkling white lights like Christmas.

Christmas morning, 1974. Rich's face mustachioed with powdered sugar from the donuts he put out for Santa Claus the night before. We wake up Dad, who still sleeps only on the left side of the bed even though Mom's been dead for two years. We run down the stairs into the dark basement where we've set up the tree, Dad following with his cup of coffee. He counts down from 10, flips the switch and the tree blinks on.

The gift takes up half the room, and even covered with the wrapping paper its shape is unmistakable: a canoe. Then Rich tearing the paper, clapping his hands, sitting in the stern, paddling air.

Tomorrow's your big day," I say after dinner, walking past the closed stores. Rich trails behind, stepping through puddles the rain has left. I keep to his right side so he can see me. "Gerry's gonna miss it."

He bends to tighten the laces of his Bean boots, my Christmas gift to him last year, and says, "Larold, old Gerry . . . she didn't make no cake, did she?"

"I don't know. Maybe she'll have one waiting for you when you get back." I'd asked her to come, but she insisted the two of us go alone. "You boys need this time together, Larry," she said, drying her hands on her apron. "Besides, it'll give me a chance to go through Richard's room with the vacuum. And it'll give you a chance to fish that river again. God knows your father loved that old river." Then why'd he sell the damned cabin? I wanted to shout. Before we drove off, I invited her again, but we both knew the gesture for what it was.

Rich says, "Larold, I'm gonna be 40 . . . 30 . . . ."

"Thirty-two," I say, pulling him up. "You're catching up to me."

"I'll catch you, Larold." He pats his pockets, looking for the pipe. "I think I left it at home . . . at the house, Larold . . . the big house."

"Let's go get it then," I say. He does a quick twist, his arms working like the Rock-em-Sock-em Robots we played with when we were kids.

When we get back to the B&B, Judy has the living room lit up like a church, dozens of candles going on the mantel and tables. Rich goes upstairs to find his pipe. Judy brings out a pot of water for herbal tea. She's a sturdy-looking woman with ruddy cheeks, and reminds me of Mary, a poet friend from Iowa. She's got the same way of making everything sound amusing, and from the look of the peonies in the beds out front she's got the same green thumb. "Have you met anyone nice in Narragansett?" I hear Gerry asking. "God knows you never talked about any girls when you were in Iowa."

"Your brother fish today, too?" Judy says, pouring the water.

"Just me. Rich fell asleep under the willows. I think he was tired from the drive."

"Asleep under the willows isn't a bad way to spend the day." Even though she says it so it sounds funny, I feel like a heel, like I've dragged my retarded brother up to Vermont just so I can go fly-fishing.

"Yeah, I suppose so," I say.

"Well, maybe he'll want to fish tomorrow," she says on her way out, her fruity perfume trailing after her. Steam rises out of the tea. Rich's boots come clunking down the stairs. Out in the woods behind the house, a barred owl asks Who-cooks-for-you?

Late in the night, Rich's steady breathing in the dark, the sound of sleep, the sound he made the day I blinded him. When it happened, the woods went suddenly silent. No sound but Rich breathing, my heart galloping into a wild panic. It was as if the birds and frogs and cicadas knew enough not to sing at a thing so terrible. The ground I stood on seemed to fly away. Our swords melted back to the dangerous sharpened sticks they were, mine tipped with what I couldn't deny. We ran through the woods toward home. "We were only playing! We were only playing!" But no matter how many times I shouted it, I couldn't make Dad look at me, couldn't make Rich's left eye come back to life. Even after the wound healed the unseeing eye was there to remind me, and it got so that I didn't want him following me around. Wasn't it then that he started acting out—breaking windows, running off and getting lost, starting fires in the field? Wasn't it then that I began hearing the whisperings, seeing Dad on the phone talking about a "special" school? And afterward, when Rich was gone, Dad on the phone with the real estate agent, describing the cabin. Maybe it wasn't about money at all. Maybe the cabin was just a sore reminder of better times. I still see Dad handing over the keys. Twenty years ago, but I see it like it was yesterday. I see it again, in the dark, with both eyes open.

The morning coffee is good and hot, and when the pancakes come Rich's stack is lit with birthday candles; Judy and I sing almost in key. I'm still not over the shock of his completely shaving his beard this morning. Even after he blows out the candles his shaven face keeps glowing.

"Happy birthday, brother," I say, handing him the wrapped package.

"Larold, is it a wallet? Is it a wallet, Larold?"

I pour more syrup onto the best cakes I've ever eaten. "Go on and open it."

He tears open the box, lifts out the meerschaum. "A pipe, a white pipe . . . I needed a new one, Larold."

"The tobacconist said it comes from Turkey. The white will gradually turn tan or brown. It breaks easy, though, so you gotta be careful, okay? And don't smoke it in bed. That'll make Gerry happy."

"For keeps, Larold? For keeps?" He sucks air through the pipe, and laughs.

"For keeps," I say.

Mid-afternoon and in the bright sun the river is ablaze with tumbling light. Nothing rising, so I'm fishing cross-stream with a Hare's Ear, mending upstream as it drifts. Rich is up on the road taking Polaroids of the red covered bridge, half the reason we stopped here in West Arlington on our way to look for the old cabin. Suddenly, there's an Eastern bluebird 20 feet away, perched on the tip of an ailanthus, and I forget about the line to watch him. But the current sets the hook, and Rich must hear the drag because he's hooting somewhere behind me. I play the fish slowly, even though it's the first of the day, and it's not until I scoop it with the net that I see it's a big brookie, red spots like blood on his flanks. When I turn around Rich is knee-deep, wearing the spare set of waders, his stained teeth grinning. "Larold! You got one!"

"Come see! Walk slow around those rocks," I say. Come see.

"Hold on, Larold. Is it deep?" But he's still grinning, he's still wading out.

"No, you can make it."

"You think I can hack it?"

"No problem." And then he's there, holding onto my arm, looking in his clean-shaven profile so much like Dad that I don't want him to let go.

"Should we keep him?" I say, but I already know that I won't. It's a day of beginnings, not endings.

"Larold, I don't know, I don't know," he says.

"I know what Dad would do." And so the two of us hold the fish gently, rocking him back and forth to revive him before letting him go.

letter from yellowstone

Peter Fong

I remember Yellowstone in 1978 the way the snake remembers Eden: like a good dream shortchanged, heaven in flames, a paradise ruined through my own corruption. So you of all people should understand why I have to go back every year. You knew Laurie then, loved her too, I suppose, though we never spoke of it, never negotiated the right or honest approach to love. You stood beside me on the sun-warmed dock at Grant Village, both of us in our Y.P. Co. uniforms, and watched her dive into Yellowstone Lake to swim with the otters, the water barely 50 degrees in July. And you watched her bite the head off a wriggling 12-inch cutthroat and casually spit the head into a bucket, the way an ordinary person might spit out a watermelon seed. And you watched her climb the last few hundred feet of Avalanche Peak in a lightning storm, then dare us to follow her by flying her shirt from one outstretched arm, like a signal flag.

You might even have married her had I not been desperate enough to quit the best job of my life three weeks early to drive with her to New Jersey for her sister's wedding. After 64 hours in a borrowed Volkswagen, listening to her rave about the splendor of rugby and the sanctity of marriage and tarpon on a fly, I forgot all about friendship. When it was my turn to drive, I spent most of the time stealing sidelong glances at the passenger seat, admiring the play of headlights in her hair, watching her face grow softer with sleep, and making plans to transfer three years of credits to the university in her home town, Missoula.

And now she's gone to Costa Rica with some Orvis-endorsed guide from Livingston, to stalk permit on the flats and—as she says—to wander her options. Isn't it sad that after 15 years of more-or-less congenial divorce, it still hurts that she didn't ask me first? It's been that kind of summer in Missoula: a late June frost, then an early August one. The tomatoes turned directly from green to black, and the snap beans produced only one meager crop. I couldn't seem to find time for the river, or when I did I was so frantic to catch trout that I pulled the fly from their mouths. Laurie's phone call raised a welt like one of those interstate bees that crashes into your bare forearm at highway speed, bumbles weakly inside the cab for a few seconds, then recovers just enough to sting you under the chin before escaping into the slipstream.

She was cheerful as always, as sure of her good intentions as on that April morning when she announced that she'd bought a house in Livingston and would be moving there with Marina the following week, and that it would probably be easier on me if I didn't help them pack. I put down the phone and walked to the Clark Fork to catch my breath. At the confluence with the Bitterroot, two sandhill cranes lumbered over the bare-limbed cottonwoods—necks up, legs down, struggling like swimmers past their depth.

I haven't recovered. For 15 years, I've been trying not to prepare for the death of hope. Every few months we have a family dinner at Chico Hot Springs or Sir Scott's Oasis. Every August we fish together on a favorite stretch of the Madison just inside the park boundary, and on those river days I can almost forget that we share only a family history, no present, no future, no geography. But her recent cheerfulness had a new lilt, an unnerving musicality that reminded me of our honeymoon in Alaska, the note of triumph as she'd set the hook in a steelhead bright from Prince William Sound. I was already facing the prospect of winter without my stock of beans canned with dill weed and jalapeños, without trout in the freezer, without tomatoes dried on the picnic table and bottled in olive oil. If Laurie was in love again, and not with me, then where was I to go?

So I called Marina, the daughter we named after the old boatyard at Grant Village, a sophomore now at Montana State and seasonal waitress at Roosevelt Lodge, where you and I used to sit in the big rockers with our feet on the porch rail, sipping gin drinks and looking out over the sagebrush until the smell of barbecued ribs and baked beans almost overcame us. I asked her to meet me at Chico on Friday night so that we could drive into the park together. She agreed with all of the cheerfulness inherited from her mother, and then I closed my eyes and saw two 20-year-old shadows close together under the lodgepole pines: the shadow that might have been you, and the shadow that almost certainly was Laurie, her face lifted for a kiss.

Arrived Chico at midnight Friday, bearing 200 miles of hunger and a hectic month's worth of exhaustion. The kitchen had closed promptly at 10, and the dining-room staff had just finished eating the last of the night's unordered desserts. They looked pleased with their work—and only mildly apologetic. Lucky for me, Marina and her friends had saved a few morsels from their plates, wrapped in aluminum foil fashioned into the shape of swans. A medallion of beef, a sliver of venison, four miniature spears of asparagus, the wing and breast of a quail.

That held me to morning. After breakfast we turned south underneath Emigrant Peak and headed for the park, Marina beside me in the pickup and a present from her affixed to the inside of the windshield—an employee's entrance pass, silhouette of a white pelican beneath the word "Yellowstone." As we hit the curves for Yankee Jim Canyon, I felt that familiar dizzy feeling—a sort of vertigo almost—when the truck seems to be rolling downhill while the road is most definitely moving uphill, against the falling river. I only feel that way in two places: on Highway 191 from the Gallatin Gateway to West Yellowstone, and on US 89 from Livingston to Gardiner. Perhaps it's because I know that I'll soon be in the park, a sort of premeditated giddiness that goes along with any return to a beloved place or person.

On that day the Yellowstone was running dirt-brown from a thunderstorm in the Lamar Valley and the sky was filled with pelicans, wheeling like oversize gulls in a great flock above the road. We craned our necks to see them as they passed over the windshield, their enormous wings flashing silver against the blue. They seemed drunk with flight, with the power to float unhindered on thin air. When we reached the stone arch outside the north entrance, a pronghorn skipped across the pavement as if possessed with that same power, each long leap more like a prelude to flight than an earthbound gait, the whole meadow like a runway.

I was sorry that you weren't there, really I was. Sorry that you couldn't feel the insane satisfaction it gave me to pass through the gate with an employee's sticker on my windshield. To shift into second gear for the twisting climb to Mammoth that we made so many times with Laurie between us. Each switchback in that road was like a pleasant surprise—a surprise because I had memories for each one, and a pleasure because I remembered.

We fished Slough Creek that afternoon, taking turns with the one rod that I brought from Missoula, an old 5-weight with a willowy mid-section that's just right for daydreaming your way through a reach of pools and riffles. I dropped Marina at Roosevelt in time for her evening shift, then headed south toward Lake Hotel, brimful with the good fortune that is my daughter.

On the way up Dunraven I got caught behind a motor yacht trolling for scenery at a leisurely 15 knots. Instead of trying to pass, I laid off the accelerator and rolled down the windows. The hillsides below the summit of Mount Washburn were already tinged with the red of autumn. At 8,000 feet the air smelled of fall, crisp and cool and faintly dusty, without the scent of growing things. To the east: the hulks of Druid Peak and the Thunderer glowering in the smoke of a late-season fire. To the south: forests of pine and fir like a ragged pelt on the flanks of the mountain, meadow grass gone golden with August, the Yellowstone River meandering through the Hayden Valley and, creeping alongside the river, the glint of aluminum travel trailers in the setting sun.

Their sheepish procession reminded me of another day of fishing with Marina, on a stretch of the Madison that runs alongside the highway to West Yellowstone, when she was still in diapers and her mother still kissed me awake in the mornings. It was a warm, breezy afternoon and I was wading wet, flipping a big caddis nymph into the deep runs while Marina watched over my shoulder from the safety of the baby pack. As we worked our way downstream, a cow elk walked out into the water below us, her neck and ears twitching with flies. She dipped her muzzle in the water, tossed her head at the shimmering surface, scratched at her neck with one sharp hoof. In minutes the road was lined shoulder to shoulder with license plates from Illinois and Washington and California.

Camera shutters shirred like locusts. The cow took a couple of prancing steps toward the far bank and shook with annoyance. Marina and I turned our backs to the crowd and kept fishing. I heard a splash nearby and to the right, like the swirl of a trout, and pivoted on the mossy rocks. "Did you hear that?" I asked her. "Was that a fish?"

"No," she said, then fell silent. I cast, letting the fly drift under a bathtub-size patch of river weed and into a dark hole of water.

I was picking up the fly to cast again when Marina whimpered: "My sandal." I repeated the word dumbly to myself—sandal, sandal—before remembering the nearby splash. I reached behind me and tickled her right foot. It was bare. When I finally looked downstream, her sandal was bobbing 20 yards away and gaining speed, on a collision course with a fully grown and fully aggravated cow elk. I tried a couple of quick shuffling steps in that direction, then sent the fly out after it. But the beloved sandal was a small, rapidly dwindling target that changed course with each little finger of current. I threw a couple of big mends into the line and still missed by a foot.

Marina's whimpering was more insistent now: "Get sandal, get sandal." I took another look at the elk and decided she wouldn't much appreciate two humans churning downstream into her bath. So I made for shore and the camera-wielding tourists, charged up the bank, then shouldered my way onto the path that parallels the river. The wind was blowing up and across the current, slowing the sandal's progress enough for us to pull ahead, but also angling it into the deeper water midstream. Fifty yards behind the elk, I picked a gravely spot and splashed in. The river was belt high. Frightened trout fled for cover as we thrashed through ribbons of weed. My feet had just reached the lip of a dark trough when the sandal floated into arm's reach. I leaned over and gathered it in like a catcher pulling an outside pitch back toward the strike zone. Marina thrust her hands into the air and cheered loud enough to turn a few cameras from the elk. I cheered too. The nearest onlookers gave us those benign and disconnected smiles that most folks reserve for fools and crazy people. But what did we care? We were flush with success, proud conspirators in a small but significant victory.

I remember wishing that Laurie could have been there to share it, but she had decided to work upstream with a brace of dry flies, toward the junction of the Gibbon and the Firehole, and later only rubbed Marina's head in a distracted sort of way when we tried to describe the scene. Then she asked about you, wondered aloud why you never wrote, and said that she could never come to the park without thinking of that summer we met.

Hard to believe that we came here in 1978 with nothing but our fly rods and a jar of tartar sauce, two college roommates from Philadelphia, babes in the woods. Is it guilt that makes me scan the faces at every fishing hole and geyser basin, looking for the wisps of blond hair feathered shyly over those raptor's eyes, your shoulders hunched slightly, as if preparing for flight? I looked for you in the fall of 1982, when a September snow blanketed our favorite camp at Heart Lake; in the smoke of 1988, when that tangle of lodgepoles upstream from Tower Falls burned right to the bank; and in the drought of 1994, when the river showed its bone-smooth black rock and water-polished deadfalls left gleaming three feet above the ordinary water line.

If you had been here you would've noticed the changes. The marina at Grant Village is long gone, only the two breakwaters to remind you of otters swimming sleekly from dock to dock. The tackle store where Laurie played cashier is now a waterfront steakhouse, and the meadow above the lake has been replaced with a hotel and restaurant complex, where you can order herbed chicken breasts and chilled Chardonnay. Our favorite stretch of the Yellowstone River, above Tower Falls, has become a certified hot spot, recommended at fly shops and touted in guidebooks. On a typical summer day the parking lot overflows with rental cars and motor homes for at least 100 yards uphill of the Hamilton store, forcing traffic to a crawl. The trail to the base of the falls has been redone with post-and-pole fences to keep over-enthusiastic sightseers from cutting switchbacks. What you might remember as a claustrophobic stand of lodgepoles crisscrossed with downed timber is now mostly open, with tremendous views of sulfur-tinged canyon walls and blue-green water. There are no longer enough shadows to hide the bears that we imagined lurked in wait for college students, and no longer enough privacy to entice those students to roast trout on a stick over a small, smoky fire. There are still a few trees left, of course, as well as some charred snags and tangles of wild roses, but a two-foot-wide path now parallels the bank for miles upstream. At every obvious pool, other paths split off the main trail and head for the river's edge. The last time I walked it, the water seemed as blank and lifeless as a mirror. I would cast, the fly would drift aimlessly with the current, no trout would move to break the surface, then I would cast again.

I let that pattern of failure repeat itself for several hours, thinking of Laurie gone and the trout too, thumbing through my book of failings like a sorry preacher with his Testament, snatching the fly from the water lest a fish hook itself and break the spell. As had become my habit in the months after Laurie took Marina with her to Livingston, I told myself that I deserved every blow that bad luck could deliver, that I had no right to expect something good to come from the way I'd acted, although of course something had. Did you know that I was in love with her—not afterward, I'm sure that you guessed afterward, but before? On that night of her farewell party, that night when I saw the two of you underneath the lodgepoles, just beyond the reach of the firelight, when I announced that I suddenly needed to go back to Philadelphia and would catch a ride with Laurie if she didn't mind? What matters, I suppose, is that I knew—or thought I knew—that you loved her, and that I waded in anyway, and now that river has washed me here, a thin stick of dead wood drifting in the current.

I continued to flog myself with those thoughts all that long afternoon, and to flail pointlessly at the water, until at last a little gray caddis flew up underneath my sunglasses and I had to stop to wipe my eyes. After that, I could no longer ignore the hordes of caddis on the bankside willows and thickets of wild rose. I tied on a caddis emerger and turned back downstream, this time paying attention to all the little pockets and eddies that others might overlook. I lingered a while in each one, steering the fly through the deeper cuts and then slowly raising it to the surface, like a swimmer nonchalantly looking for air. More often than not, the shadow of a trout rose after it, looming into view like a ribbon of gold in the green water. No monsters came to the fly, but the action was steady and the fish beautiful, with sleek flanks and a firm, limber strength that trout raised in warmer, slower water can't pretend to own.

Back at the confluence of Tower Creek and the Yellowstone, I looked longingly at the sharp, steep bend in the canyon wall, no trail visible in the soft earth. Since the river was low, I figured I could sneak along the ankle-deep ledge and get downstream to the more lightly fished water. But the afternoon sun was wearing on into evening, and the back of my throat was dust-dry, and the image of a double-dip ice cream cone suddenly appeared in my head and remained there, perfectly frozen. I snipped off the tattered emerger, stowed my reel in a vest pocket and started up the hill.

On the canyon rim two mighty tour buses had just pulled into the parking lot and disgorged their charges. The trail was flooded with mothers, fathers, children, grandmothers. Judging from the conversation, they were mostly Americans, though I also caught snatches of accented English that reminded me how little I know of the world. Inside the Hamilton store, the line for ice cream wound up and down the aisles like a New Year's parade. I swallowed hard and bought a six-pack instead.

Drank dinner last night in the high-ceilinged lobby at Lake Hotel, gazing out the picture window while a string quartet sawed away at the evening. Do you remember the time some Park Service employees dug a charcoal pit in the gravel beach near Fishing Bridge, buried a whole pig in the hot coals, then got too drunk to eat and just left the carcass roasting in the sand? By the time we stumbled onto the scene, only a half-dozen stout souls were still awake, lounging against two unopened cases of barbecue sauce while the stars spun in their orbits. I can still see you and Laurie pulling the succulent meat from the bones, as soft and sweet as cotton candy, while white-winged pelicans ghosted across the full moon like pterodactyls.

For some reason, that memory made it impossible for me to eat or sleep. I lay awake all night remembering how happy we felt, how impossibly lucky to roam the beach of Yellowstone Lake under a full moon in July and catch the scent of keg beer and slow-cooked meat. At that time I thought that it had everything to do with the three of us together, but now I recall that Laurie had rousted us from our beds after midnight, just to share the moon, and neither one of us could resist her.

In the morning, I checked out before breakfast and drove southwest along the lake shore, then turned west along the Grand Loop Road to cross and recross the Continental Divide. A cold front had blown the smoke out of the park and the western horizon looked sharp and blue. I fought the urge to turn in at Old Faithful for a Bloody Mary at the Bear Pit, stopping instead at the Lower Geyser Basin, taking the bridge over the Firehole and making my way through the crowds to the end of the boardwalk. As I peered into the crater of Fountain Geyser, an old man in a soft canvas hat, a disposable camera dangling from his leathery neck, croaked, "It's gonna blow." Sure enough, several standing waves appeared in the turquoise pool, then a tidal surge, and then the sky filled with steam and water, great blasts that frothed 30 feet into the air, splashed onto a flood plain of white sinter, then ran downslope to pool about the hooves of grazing bison. Above the slosh and grumble of the geyser, I could hear the shouts of children, cheering with each burst of water as if they were riding in the front seat of a roller coaster. For a moment I wished that Marina was small again, riding in the baby pack with her warm arms around my neck, until I remembered the deft motion with which she unhooked a 16-inch rainbow without lifting it from the water, then stood straight-backed again and smiling, a loop of line already rising into the air. Maybe next year, I thought, we'll take our own trip south—to Belize maybe, or the southern Yucatan.

We'd even invite Laurie, if she wanted to go, and I could watch the two of them stalk bonefish and marvel at both the one who used to love me and the one who always will.

By the time the geyser roared itself dry again, I was hungry. I drove straight into West Yellowstone and bought a bag of cocktail shrimp, a hunk of blue cheese, a loaf of sourdough bread and a flask of bourbon. I spent the rest of the afternoon prospecting the Madison, fishing off-handedly upstream until I encroached on another angler or strayed too far from the bourbon and the shrimp chilling in the cooler. By sunset I had worked my way to within a mile of the junction, where the river meanders weedily through a broad meadow of sedge and thistles.

As soon as I parked the truck, two cow elk and their calves crossed the river above me and bent their necks to graze. I had an hour of twilight left and knotted a black marabou fly as long as my thumb to the leader. Big fish or no fish. I dropped the fly alongside the shadowed banks and inched it leechlike toward the main current; flipped it behind boulders and under deadfalls; cast it into the current and pulsed it back toward the bank. No sign of trout. As I splashed through a backwater to the next bend, a 10-inch rainbow fled before me, pushing a small wake that creased the fading light. Twenty yards farther downstream, a frightened minnow skittered into the air and fell back again. I watched for the tell-tale swirl of a big brown but saw nothing, gave the pool a couple dozen careful casts just in case. Still nothing. I stood in the middle of what seemed like a lifeless pool while the water broke behind my knees and rejoined below them, a soft sound that I suddenly wished would drown the endless thrum of cars on the road to West Yellowstone, travelers turned away from the park's chock-full hotels or employees out for a night on the town.

I fished hard for a while, casting steadily, moving two steps downstream with each cast. The dark crept into the water first, so that slick moss and shallow gravel and shoulder-deep holes all began to look dimly alike. The rush of engines grew louder and the glare of headlights brighter. I snipped the fly from my tippet and wound the leader onto the reel. When I shuffled at last to shore, the elk had worked in behind me.

If you will forgive me, I thought, I will abstain from fishing tomorrow, and from catching and killing fish, and forgo the satisfaction of watching that delicate orange meat of a Yellowstone cutthroat flake from the bones.

The nearer cow picked up her head and turned her big ears toward my sigh. Not the worried, ready-to-bolt look of elk in hunting season, but a gesture of interest. Her calf took two bouncing steps then melted in behind her, aligning legs with her mother's so that they seemed to become a single alert and yet unconcerned animal. I spoke to them, quiet reassurances and words of small praise. They were beautiful. A half-mile upstream, I could see the bleached shell of the pickup glowing in the pale light of the moon.

spanish fly

Kent Cowgill

C all me Pedro." The words seemed innocent enough at the time, merely the latest of his harmless quirks, like his taste for goat cheese or the occasional pitcher of sangria. But they loom now, looking back, as Pete Smith's private Niagara—the moment he went over the edge.

When I saw him next, a month later, he was working an evening midge hatch on the Madison. He'd pulled his hair back into a tight pigtail. A pair of new black neoprenes stretched over his rawbone frame, sheathing it like a body condom. And where a dinged canteen had bounced for years, a goatskin bota dangled against his lean flanks.

"What the hell's got into him?" Clyde croaked that night as we sat hunched over our vises in his den. "The bastard looks like he just got off a bus from Juarez."

I didn't respond, intent on palmering a webby length of hackle over a dyed hank of roadkill coyote. "Beats me," I finally said, still locked in on the embryo streamer emerging under my jittery fingers. The shape and color of a stick of dynamite, it was destined to hit the water as the Big Wile E.

"A shrink would have a field day with that guy," I added, snipping off a wayward guard hair. "He's getting weirder all the time."

Wally nodded and slid off his stool. "I need another brew," he said, heading for the kitchen.

Clyde squinted at his disappearing back. "*Cerveza,*" he growled, his arthritic digits bent around a hot-pink swatch of woodchuck ear hair. "Bring me one of 'em too."

"Serve you what?" Wally said, turning back. His oval face furrowed in the light of the refrigerator door.

"Another beer," I said. "Disregard the Clydester. Whatever bug bit Pete must have got a piece of him too."

"Are you nuts?" Clyde shot back. "I was just repeatin' the only word I've heard from him lately where I had some idea what he was sayin'. What the hell's a tacos bar, anyway?"

The old plumber shook his head in disgust. Tufts sprouted like centipede legs from under his thumb, fringing the hook wrapped with elastic from one of his ex-wife's garter belts. Over the years I'd seen him tie the gaudy nymph by the boxful, swearing he'd quit the day he extracted one from a fish's lip. The bibulous night of his divorce, when he'd created it, he'd christened it the Ovar 'n Dun.

"Tapas bar," I corrected him. "It's a bar that serves food," I said. "He told me they're big in Spain. Like all the other stuff he's gotten into lately. You've heard him. Flamenco. Paella. Classical guitar."

The baggy eyes rolled toward the ceiling as the tying thread snapped under a horny nail.

"Far as I'm concerned, it's all a bunch of bull," he groaned.

"That too," Wally said.

A few weeks later the four of us were out again, on bigger water, and the season had changed. The aspens had turned golden and the cottonwoods had begun to drop their leaves in the gunmetal runs and the riffles that shimmered in the autumn wind like plates of silver. Pete leaped out of the van before the motor died and shambled off into the pines, his tote bag slung over his rod case. The raven hair he hadn't cut for months fell in long raffish strands down his shoulders. His nostrils flared like a rutting deer's.

When he strode out of the trees 10 minutes later, he carried the graphite rod like a lance, a small wedge-shape hat crowning the newly braided pigtail. An embroidered vest rode stiffly over his shirt and he'd donned a thin black tie that made his lean frame look even thinner. Or maybe he was thinner; it was hard to tell.

"God almighty," Clyde puffed, pulling on his hippers beside me. "What the hell's he gone and done now?"

It took some time before I could answer.

"I don't know," I finally said, transfixed. "He's been reading a lot lately, I know that . . . . I saw him come out of the library when I drove by last weekend. He had about a dozen books in his arms."

"Goddamn," the plumber repeated, grinding the butt of his cigar into the sand. "When I first met him, he sold bathroom fixtures. And most of the fish he caught were on a Number 3 Mepps."

"He still sells bathroom fixtures," I said.

Slowly donning my own gear, I watched as Pete strode past with his eyes narrowed, his belly flat and his dark face creased and tight like the skin of a walnut. The face worried me until I looked at it closer and then it worried me more.

Wally stood beside me, gaping like a top-feeding carp. We watched as Pete entered the river. He splashed on past a gravel bar either of us would have claimed to cast into the calf-deep riffle above it, slowing his pace only when the dark folds of water lapped hard and threateningly against his thighs. Leaning into the current for balance, he fumbled for his fly box, thin as a cigarette case inside the pocket of his blue spangled vest. His privates bulged like a ballet dancer's. The new neoprenes glinted like a coal seam in the sun.

A fly somehow appeared in his hand as the surging current swept him downstream—spun him through a funnel of whitewater in a pair of twinkling pirouettes around his Fenwick. But he didn't go down.

"How did he do that?" Wally whispered. "Holy God!"

"He's always had great balance," I murmured. "But that was the best I've ever seen."

We stared even more intently as he knotted on the fly, trying to catch a glimpse of the pattern he had chosen. Pete's eyes narrowed as they moved over the water, reading its bumps and bulges, and I was sure there hadn't been much left to pick from the once-encyclopedic ranks lining his box. A week earlier, through a sleepless night in his cramped bachelor flat, he'd pared it down with the sweating zeal of a weight-shedding wrestler, discarding both flies and the books where he'd learned to tie them until dawn broke over the outcast tomes. Everything published after the advent of Flashabou had been jettisoned around midnight. He'd apparently come to rest at four or five in the morning over the broken spines of Swisher and Richards, his shelves bare of all but John Alden Knight and Joe Brooks.

"Whaddaya think he's goin' with?" Wally murmured beside me. "Nothin's risin', and if he ain't lyin' he's chucked most of his nymphs and all his attractors and streamers . . . . I still don't have a clue why."

"He got rid of anything he thought was 'tricked-up,'" I said. "'*Trucos*,' he called them. He told me every time he opened his box and saw them staring back at him, it felt like he'd opened the door of a cheap hotel room and seen something lewd."

"So what's he got left?" the mailman mumbled, shaking his head.

"Not much," I said. "A few mayfly imitations. One or two Cowdungs. At least one Royal Coachman I know he's got stashed away somewhere."

"I still don't get it," he said, his round eyes blinking behind his wire-rim glasses. "The Coachman's about as gaudy as a fly gets. It's gotta be one of them trucos."

"You're right," I continued. "But when I picked him up this morning he dug it out of the trash can just before he closed the door. It wasn't pretty. The way he looked reminded me of a man falling off the wagon, reaching for a fifth of Scotch."

Wally pulled out his handkerchief and blew his nose.

"I guess it's not that surprising, if you think about it," he said. "When he was just gettin' started the Coachman was all he ever used."

"It was the fly that hooked him," I said and nodded as I remembered. "I suppose it's about as close as feathers come to a red-and-white Mepps."

We continued to watch. Clyde clumped back up the bank past us, shaking his head as he disappeared around the bend.

Pete had inched out even farther into the river. It humped and thrust at his loins as he arched his back, stripped line and began casting toward an upstream eddy. A shadow fell across the water. Banks of clouds were rolling in from the mountains, sealing off the sun.

"If we're gonna do any fishing ourselves, we better get goin'," Wally murmured. "Look at that sky."

A half-hour later we were still watching Pete. He hadn't had a strike and no fish were working and the freshening wind had blurred our eyes and put a steady run in Wally's nose. It was the casting that held us—the dance of his rod painting the water in a cascade of feathery kisses and curls. He made long casts. Short casts. Casts to parts of the river a trout might last have visited a generation earlier. He made roll casts. Wind cheaters. Switch pickups and negative curves. And then, still fishless, he began to blanket the river with casts I knew only because one night, when I'd driven by and seen him in the back alley practicing in the moonlight, I sneaked into his room and checked his latest books.

The rhythms of his rod kept burning away their yellowed pages—fired them into art as we watched. His casts flowed to closure so hypnotically I heard my lips murmuring the reverent words he'd been whispering when I'd left his room and crept up behind him that night under the moon. His eulogy to "Mr. Charles Ritz of Paris, France" who "threw a bow so tight" the faded photographs still hit you "like a cornada cut through the heart."

And so the two of us kept watching him, our eyes fogged with wonder. Beside me, Wally's rod hung limp in his hand.

And finally Pete hooked a fish. It was a small fish, no more than 12 inches, but it was a thick-shouldered brown and it fought bravely, and it came to hand with bright speckled sides glinting in the sun. Pete arched over the rod, motionless, his back ramrod straight and his legs together. He released it with a single deft flick of the barbless hook, then turned abruptly away from the wild river's roar.

Bouncing joyously out of the run, he splashed across the gravel bar to stand, vest and tie dripping, on a flat rock a few feet from where we stood. The bota hung where he'd left it, looped over a willow. Hoisting it above his head, he squeezed a spurt of the dribbling wine toward his open throat and bit it off savagely as the still-jetting stream sluiced down his chin.

Wally wiped his nose with the back of his hand, eyeing him warily. Pete's eyes looked like a pair of white marbles glazed in a kiln.

None of us said anything for some time.

"Man, oh man," Wally finally ventured. "That was awesome. You're doin' stuff I've never seen anybody else do out there."

Pete said nothing. Hung the goatskin back on the willow. Turned slowly and stared out at the shoulders of current bulging darkly under the lowering sky.

"The maximum of exposure," he murmured. "The purity of line."

He stepped toward the water.

This time he waded even farther out than before. The current beat now a few inches below his ribcage. Coils of line unfurled like the locks of Medusa on the slick water behind him as he stripped them from his reel.

A light snow had begun to sift out of the sky, flecking the tight warp of his wool hat, but the soundless casts again shot long and true across the wind-whipped water. The fly landed daintily at the top of the run, near the headstone boulder—a dark V where the current split into a pair of deep chutes that funneled menacingly toward him 30 yards below.

My hands had stiffened in the cold but I stood watching, following the blaze-orange line, its tracery sliding like a tongue of flame over the river. He was still a little quick, I thought, remembering the old Pete. Still just a shade limp-wristed. But the strides he'd made since I'd last seen him fish were as astonishing as the matador hat and spangled vest he wore. Somehow, it all began to fit. I was no aficionado, but to my amateurish eye each cast looked cleaner than the one that preceded it. The arcing rod seemed to bend the brawling river to its will.

Behind me, I heard Clyde stumble up to join us. He was gasping—whether from the exertion of hauling his girth up the sandy bank or from the spectacle riveting his own snow-fringed orbs I was too absorbed to check. Pete had edged out even farther; he stood now on his toes, casting to the glassy lie behind the boulder. His black-hatted frame loomed through the snow like an apparition glimpsed through a veil.

On the third or fourth cast he appeared to roll a fish, but he hooked nothing. Ten minutes later he stood beside us on the shore.

"By God, that's a big one," he crowed. "Big *bicho*. He's holding in his *querencia*. I can't get him to work." Lighting a cigarette, he took two or three short stabbing puffs before flicking it disdainfully into the river. The butt spun downstream past him as he splashed again out over the bar. Clyde stared at his departing back, muttered something I didn't catch as he headed for the Bronco. Wally and I stood where we were, peering through the snow.

"He is nuts," Wally said. "Clyde's right. The dude's about three aces shy of a full deck."

Staring numbly at his rod, he began to break it down. "But I got to say this for him," he added. "He's for damn sure been gettin' somethin' out of all them books of his . . . . Makes me think I shouldn't of dropped out of school."

I didn't get out with Pete again until the next season, after the spring runoff had spent itself and the water had cleared enough so you could glimpse pebbles on the bottom. I'd seen him a few times during the winter, mostly through the ice-glazed window of his apartment, bent so intently over his desk I didn't feel inclined to stop and disturb his reveries. I did look up "querencia" in a Spanish dictionary. Learned it's the place in a bullring where a bull feels safest.

When we finally did make it out on the river, Wally came too, despite the fact he had to take a sick day from the post office to do it. Clyde feigned a grumbling host of reservations, but I knew in the end he'd be waiting on his porch with his thermos of Irish coffee and his battered rod case.

I had volunteered to drive, to pick Pete up at dawn, hoping the few minutes alone with him driving across town would give me a jump on the questions we all had about his latest visions. The first answer wasn't long in coming. "What river do you want to fish?" I asked as we idled at a stoplight, peering out at the first faint pink streaks in the sky.

He slowly turned from the window at the words, a thin smile creasing his face, jolted out of some private musing. Shaking a cigarette out of his crumpled pack, he stared at it for a long moment before lighting it, finally responding in syllables so soft and distant they hung like the shroud of blue smoke in the air.

"There is but one, my friend," he murmured. "The rest are *nada*. The day of the Bighorn has come."

An hour later Wally and I stood on its north bank with our rods strung. This time Clyde remained with us, waiting. He'd muttered under his breath, rolled his eyes, whenever Pete's name came up over the winter, but we all knew the odds he'd strike off downriver and miss whatever was about to happen were roughly the same as his coming up with another garter belt from his ex-wife. If anything, he looked even more expectant than Wally, whose fireside tales of what he had missed the last time out had turned more than one of our winter tying sessions into concerts of bearish grunts and growls of disbelief.

Pete had directed us to a ranch that flanked the river—a roaring stretch of water where the Bighorn bent left and tumbled sharply down a gauntlet of fire-blackened pines. A ring of scorched hills formed a kind of moonscape amphitheater behind it. The short grass shone black as a sable pelt in the morning sun.

Already pigtailed, Pete climbed out and again toted his gear into a rock-cloistered changing room; it soon became clear that his winter pilgrimage had led him through a lot more shrines.

The spangled vest and hat were gone. His leaders were coiled between damp flannel pads. The orange line had been sacrificed to one of ivory. And somehow, apparently by selling most of what he owned, he'd managed to replace his rod with a matchless little Leonard whose silver fittings had been polished so lovingly they glinted between the lengths of cane like shards of cut gems.

All of which was little more than a prelude to the flies. He'd left them by the rod when he disappeared behind the rocks, and Wally had snapped open the thin box before Pete's pigtail had vanished from our view.

The once-triple-digit collection had been pared further; it now held only a single pattern—a trim hairwing I knew the name of only because he'd delivered a paean to it as we drove through the dawn-lit streets. He called it the "Papa Wulff." Told me it was a hybrid. Said he'd created it as a legacy to the two "*toros bravos*" whose streamside memories would "rise forever with the sun."

None of the flies was larger than a thumbtack. When he stepped into the water a few minutes later, he tied on the tiniest and spat on it for luck.

We watched as he moved out to where the current darted hard at his knees.

When the first cast came even Clyde could see it was flawless, and I heard him gasp behind me as the tiny fly sang over the water and dropped with the purity of a communion wafer not 10 feet from where we stood. Then the line lifted and sang again through chords of chaste backcasts that swelled into a symphony as the rod moved on over the river in a widening fan. Clyde took a lurching step forward, bumping my elbow. Wally's right hand rose in a sun-shielding salute above his eyes.

And then Pete moved farther out. A lot farther.

Far enough that the bludgeoning current suddenly bounced him downriver in a heartstopping surge that miraculously ended with his feet somehow secure behind a foam-caked, rock-wedged log. The river roared into a chute of whitewater fury just a few yards below him. My own heart was thumping like the river in my throat.

"Jesus," Wally croaked. "Jesus God."

Clyde glanced at him but said nothing. The color had drained from his face.

We watched as the casts began again, rose and slowly accelerated, spread over the river like a net. Casts so immaculate they made you forget the danger and the fire-ravaged prairie and even the raging river that gored at Pete's groin. His left leg was slightly advanced, arrow straight. His right was a shaft of sinew behind it. And the rod kept lifting as the ivory line penned lyric parabolas like a stream of scrolled ink flowing out of his hand.

When the strike came he set the hook gently, almost indolently, and played the fish off the reel. It was a fine fish and he played it cleanly as it bulled up and down in heavy surges that ended only when he released it with a quick, barely perceptible flourish of his left wrist. The rod curved above him as he executed the release, high and quivering—the bow of his arched body a mirror image of his taut right arm.

Exultant, he bounced out of the river to the relieved burst of our pent-up breath, each buffeted step punctuated by a collective gasp of foreboding. Wally cradled Pete's bota as he reached us, and he snatched it from the mailman's trembling fingers as soon as his booted foot struck the shore. This time the wine hit his throat in a crimson jet that he bit off with the finality of a slamming cell door. Swallowing hard, he wiped the sweat from his eyes, then lifted the skin again and gulped several more mouthfuls before spitting the last on the sand.

"*Cojones*," he murmured. "*Grandes huevos*. That fish had balls."

None of us said anything. Clyde pawed a trickle of tobacco juice off his grizzled chin.

And before we could reach out to restrain him, Pete had stepped back into the river, edged farther out, pirouetting on his toes as the current bumped and shouldered his bony frame toward the very throat of the narrows. I looked away as a wave of nausea washed over me. But again his feet somehow caught, found purchase on the shifting bottom. When my eyes opened on him again he stood chest deep behind a jagged rock no larger than a plowshare, its jut rising out of the dark torrent like the prow of a ship whose shattered spars trailed through 100 yards of violent water below.

Wally had dropped to his knees. I fought off the nausea once more and fixed my swimming eyes on the distant hills, where the fire line had burned out in half a dozen licking tongues of ebony. Clyde stood at my other elbow, rigid, his jaw a slab of granite frozen around the butt of his cigar.

When I looked back at the river, the casts were moving over it like the breaths of God and somewhere in the blinding sun a trout shot out of the water in a diamond tiara of spray. Pete played this one, too, off the humming reel I could just hear over the roar of the whitewater and the reverent whisper that suddenly hissed from the gravelly throat at my side.

"*Olé!*"

Numb, I turned as the big trout soared again, saw the cigar butt fall to the sand and heard the same throat cut the air with the feral ferocity of a chainsaw.

"*Olé! Olé!*"

And suddenly the tears were coursing down my cheeks too as Wally rose to his feet and his choked voice swelled to join ours in a full-throated cry over the raging river.

"*Olé! Olé! Olé!*"

Pete turned, glanced toward us as the rod shuddered in his hand, a smile lighting his face like the beatific peace of an angel. And in that split second the fish surged and the bulling river hooked Pete as his foot slipped and a few dazed eyeblinks later he was gone.

We found his body a mile downstream, grappled to a tangle of roots, afloat in a quiet pool below a shaded bank hanging grassy and low over the water. Strangely, there wasn't a mark on it. He still clutched the shattered Leonard in his palm.

edith's rule

Seth Norman

Sometimes I am sad and sometimes resentful and either way I am old, getting cranky, convinced that the bass are harder than they used to be. Especially that beast under the willow in the big pool, 543 steps downstream from the dam.

Used to be 502, which shows you how long I've been fishing this stretch, and how much time I have on my hands.

Lots of time; still, often these days I don't check in with Bud at his counter in the park office. I just don't feel like it, which means that on the way out or whenever he catches up with me—like he managed to do this morning—he dogs me, standing there staring with his Weimaraner eyes and his hearing aid perched on one ear like a slug.

"Got to let me know, sir," he said.

"Judas Priest, Bud, like you don't already? Like I'm not here seven days out of seven?"

"Not the point, sir. It's the rule and I want to know."

He was right but I glowered. "What is the point, exactly, Bud?"

No expression in those eyes. Blank. The petals of two blue flowers with a black pistil in each. But he's tuned, believe me.

"The point is that you're about the only person who fishes back in there, where there's copperheads and cottonmouths, snapping turtles bigger than you are and some rough walking, which might not be a problem if you'd only carry a stick. The point is that I do not intend to let you die slow one night because I don't know to go find you, so you sign my goddamn book, sir, every time you come in, and don't tell me again about your lifetime pass. Please, sir, and thank you."

See what I mean?

I didn't stick around after that. Doesn't matter, except that I had wanted to ask him about the girl again, and I'd half thought to show him Edith's 5-weight outfit, which I've been using lately even though it's small for my hand and too light, really, to throw bigger bugs. What a sweet little rod though, a treasure, with its slim grip still clean and unmarked because Edith would never hook her flies into the cork. "A perfect lady's rod," I might have told Bud, because that would also describe Edith. Then maybe I would have mentioned something about Edith's Rule.

Probably not. Bud doesn't actually fish much, and when he does it's with a bobber for what he calls "brim," or for crappie—a word he pronounces to rhyme with sappy, suggesting fecal fish. Anyway I probably couldn't have pulled off the "perfect lady" line without getting sappy myself: The doctor warned me that after surgeries like the one that zippered my chest, "You'll tend to find yourself more emotional, and more likely to show it."

Which with me means getting mean, apparently. Sometimes I really can't figure out where my manners have gone. Me, who thinks manners have more to do with maintaining civilization than almost any of the more vaulted ideals—suddenly I can't seem to snap my teeth fast enough to bite back exactly the kind of remark for which silence was invented.

Speaking of which: Is that girl going to be watching me today? Skulking about through the trees. Exactly how long has she been doing that?

I first noticed her last week, but she's very quiet, so who knows? I'm not even sure I heard her at all. Maybe I was just looking around, like I do more often these days, wondering where everything's gone—and there she was, standing partly hidden behind a big dogwood, maybe 75 feet away. She dropped her eyes when I squinted, then slipped away along the slope, probably on a deer trail up through there.

I didn't call to her, of course. I wouldn't have thought about her again except that I saw her near the same spot two days later, just as I was deciding which tree to irrigate—very annoying. She disappeared instantly, but I'm pretty sure I heard her close by an hour later, which means she'd been stalking me the whole time.

Bud told me her story that afternoon. He's talked to her several times or more than that. "She's 12 years old and curious, real shy, maybe tryin' to learn a few things."

I thought that was awfully damn obvious of him. I wondered if he also told her I was a ringer for Grampa Walton. "You know, Bud," I said, and I still flush to remember my tone, "I don't mind fishing alone. I don't mind it at all."

Bud stared at me, unreadable as a clock face without hands. I kept thinking he was going to say something. I don't know how I'd have responded if he did, but I suddenly felt tired and told him I was going home. Not that going home helped: All evening I worried about what Edith would have thought if she'd heard me be so rude. Got so bad I eventually took out her tackle for the first time and cleaned it up just as if it needed attention and she would forgive me.

Of course there's no reason the girl shouldn't watch, except that I don't want her to. She has every right. Bud says her people have owned the slope above the big pool—my pool, it feels like—for a hundred years, maybe two, though none of them have lived around here since anybody can remember. Or they hadn't until her mother brought in a brushhog to clear a patch up near the road, then had a trailer pulled in.

I hear her visitors sometimes, when I've stayed late of an evening. Or their cars, and maybe I see the headlights reflecting off the trees.

It happens that I'm not the one to pass judgment on these men, but it's because of them that I didn't talk to the girl yesterday when I spotted her way down near the tail of the pool. It was the right moment to address her directly, maybe even wade across to explain face-to-face that one of the most important parts of fishing to me is solitude. I should have done it and I'll have to, but the problem is that I don't want her to think that I'm saying this because her mother's a prostitute. I mean, for Christ's sake consider the grief she'll get when the junior high school opens in the fall, the subtle stuff and blatant smirks that will hit her like a slap across the mouth. It's a small town, and not without pity, but a few hard hearts can break yours when you're young, and I just don't want to be mistaken for one of those.

So maybe I won't even go all the way to the big pool today. I don't have to. Below me right here is a smaller one, a slow channel really, with half a dozen bluegill holding close to a bank where kudzu swarms down to swallow a deadfall.

Here's the choice: I could toss out a little popper—and Lord I love a popper—one of my own itty-bitty deerhair babies, which are getting hard for me to spin, or one of the store-bought foam doodads that work just as well and are cheap. (I won't fish deep this early in the day, because there will be plenty of time for streamers later.) Normally I use my own ties in the morning, when I'm still fresh and my casts correctly made more often than not, unless there's a serious reason to think I might hang a branch while taking a reasonable risk.

Like right now. If I wade to position from below and stoop enough to where it hurts my knees—some anglers don't understand how well bluegill see, how smart they've got to be to live a year—I'll have a clear shot forward. I'll also have hell with yellow pine and brambles behind, meaning a tight little rollcast—and that's why I use a double-taper line, never mind the economy of it. But a rollcast from an uncomfortable crouch, while I'm shaking a little like I do, with Edith's rod just a tad lighter than I want . . . it's sure easy to imagine that the fly will drift right into kudzu. That's okay if it tumbles off one of the broad leaves, as it probably will, acting exactly like what those tiny terrors expect of a clumsy beetle or spider or some other bug. But if the fly slips between leaves, catches down in the stems . . . .

Justifiable risk, I'd say. For a foam popper, anyway. And I would take it post haste, except for another fly—this one in the ointment. There's a reason the bluegill are grouped at the front of the channel, and it's green-backed and golden-eyed, suspended deep in the branches of that deadfall, a Sunfish Nemesis. He's not a monster bass like the one at the big pool, but I bet he's three pounds. Not bad, for a warm little tailwater nobody else bothers much.

He won't come up for a popper, though. Or I haven't been able to raise him. Maybe at night I could. Wonder if I could still manage that? Give Bud fits if he knew I tried.

The problem is that he might well come after a bluegill, if it's hooked and struggling, trying to head into cover. There's half a chance, anyway. Then it will be trumpets and drums for as long as it takes the bass to dis-gorge or to drag both bluegill and fly back into that deadfall, everything and body tangled together in a macramé of leader and branches with a live fish or two thrashing around where I can't get at them without a mask and fins.

What a mess! So, Edith, what I might do—

See there. That happens. Lots, lately—all of a sudden. It's strange, because it never did when she was alive. Didn't need to . . . this sudden sense of her, a rush of presence so immediate to me. What's stranger still, it only happens when I'm fishing, not ever when I'm alone at the house and might welcome the company, if that's what to call it.

I don't know what to think about that. Fishing for me has always meant slipping into a state of mind with borders nearly as absolute as a river bank or ocean shore. All the preparations and whatnot, the evenings with magazines or at the vise, the people you know because fishing is what you do—that's all been part of my life. But when I'm on the water the act of fishing engages me completely: Every nerve stays directed, focused. Even these days that's still so true that sometimes I'll forget about lunch until after the morning shadows falling to this bank fall back across to the other. "It's a place all your own you go to," Edith said soon after we were married, "and I don't mind at all, as long as you come home to me."

I always did. Now I would if I could.

Edith came along, of course. Not often, because she had places of her own to go. But sometimes. Always, on trips to the mountains for trout, when for a few hours at a time she'd lay out her short, picture-perfect casts, in an action that was to my own like a pirouette to putting the shot. "Now go on," she'd say after I'd watched a little. "Now you go on. I know what you want to do. I'll be here when you get back. And I'll probably still love you, though there's no guarantee you'll get dinner."

Sometimes when I returned she'd still be casting, but the cane rod I'd bought her was heavy, and she wouldn't consider any other until this one I'm using today came along. Finding it, of course, was a big surprise—the only time she ever applied Edith's Rule to herself.

I doubt I could have explained Edith's Rule to Bud if I tried. That wasn't even Edith's name for such a fine and crazy idea, which she seemed to think was just an extension of common sense—which it is, if only in the same way as the Golden Rule and most of the Ten Commandments.

The first time I saw her use it was my first year at college, after I came back from the war. We were both cubs on the newspaper staff then. I'd already half noticed her—a tiny, friendly girl with peaked eyebrows, a sly smile and wit that could sneak in and make your head snap back with laughter. Lovely, she really was, but she seemed still a girl to me and the war had put me apart from what I thought of as "kids." Then one day she brought me a framed picture in a cloth bag.

"Here," she said. "This is yours."

At first I thought it was some kind of fantastic photograph of a big-mouth bass. Then I looked closer. The image was constructed of tiny dots, almost like pixels on a comic book page, except this was hand done, with art in it, by somebody named Thomas Gonzales. Wonderful thing, really. I still hadn't put it down when I asked her what this was all about.

She laughed. "Don't make too much of it," she said. "It's just that sometimes there's a certain thing that naturally belongs to a particular person, and far and away fits them best. I've been reading your fishing stories so I know this picture belongs to you, only it happened to fall into my hands on its way."

Crazy thinking. Completely. But she wouldn't let me buy it and she wouldn't take it back, absolutely not. At first she wouldn't even let me take her to dinner, by way of making some compensation. Then she did, and we had this lifetime together after that.

Edith's Rule, I came to call this. I saw it invoked half a hundred times after that, occasionally with people almost strangers. Most folks were as baffled as I was that first time, yet you could always see by their expression that whatever Edith gave them was something they would treasure, even if they hadn't known they would—uncanny, she was. A hat or a lamp, once a set of antique crochet needles she saw at a garage sale. But I never saw her apply it to anything she wanted for herself until one day while we were on vacation near Loveland.

We'd stopped at a shop for information and to buy a few flies. The fellow was ringing me up when Edith put a rod down beside the register, a little wand of a 5-weight called an Elkhorn. "And please ring this also," Edith said.

Out of the blue—just like that. I must have opened my mouth to say something—no doubt to offer my supposedly expert opinion—but she reached up and put her finger across my lips. Then, for the first and only time, she used my name for her habit. "Edith's Rule," she whispered.

I can hear her say it now. It sounds like a breeze in these trees, and it is of course. But it makes me remember how her hand held the very grip I have in mine this instant, then the warm feel of her and of the way her body moved. Her strength. She was so slight you couldn't have guessed that she flexed like spring steel; but with a touch so tender it made me want to say "Thank you" aloud. God, I watched her watching me in the light of so many thousand nights, marveling at how everything fit, her skin smooth as slowly moving water and the seams of her small muscles shifting, folding and opening, lovely lines leading me back to her face, to her eyes. I can remember how she amazed me that first time, when I did not expect she would teach me how little I'd learned in the brothels of Bari, soon after we'd bombed Rommel into the sand and had begun flying the missions north that we all believed would kill us—so many of us were right—and had tried to seize every scrap of pleasure from a life we feared we would lose . . . .

Imagine, leaving life before Edith. Before learning that just as surely as there are things that seemed to be made for people who will well and truly love them, so are some people made for one another. Created that way, or shaped so closely that suddenly the words "You're Mine" on a Valentine's heart mean something different from possession, a recognition of belonging that is like light.

Edith.

I'm not going to cast for those bluegill. Or to that bass I can't figure out. I can't even see them, if you want to know the truth. But I'll be all right pretty soon. Certainly by the time I get to the big pool. I will be all right because fishing is my place, the place I go to. And it's fine that she visits me there.

I don't see her on the slope. The girl. She could be watching and probably is. She'll see me catch that big bass, I promise. Because I know exactly how I will—have it figured to the moment. I know what I'm going to cast and where, then how much line I will have to strip while I slowly wade back out of the fish's vision; and how long I'll wait until I've faded from its dim monster memory. Twenty minutes on the watch, then I'll give one . . . little . . . twitch.

I'll catch him all right.

But not today.

I see her now, downstream, closer than ever before. It's time to get this done.

We watch each other as I wade across. She's an ordinary girl, I should think. Worried, the way she holds her hands, perhaps sad. But I can tell by her eyes that this time she's not going away.

Probably Bud warned her. Told her that I am old and widowed, pitiful and turning mean. But I'm going to explain anyway that I only need to be left alone to find my private place, because that's what I have. She may not understand that need now. Perhaps she will someday.

I'm certain she will. Someday very soon, I'm afraid.

I say, "Young lady," and in that moment it feels like my thoughts have been severed from one another, as if by looking into her face I see sky.

"Young lady," I say again, pausing because I'm suddenly so surprised and frightened, and must drift an instant before I let go, surrender all of a rush after fighting so hard. "This is for you. It was my wife's rod. I think she would like you to have it."

The girl looks confused and she draws her hands back from her sides. I would say the rest if I could, reassure her, answer questions she cannot know to ask. But it's all I can do to wait for her to take the grip I have extended, to watch as her stare is distracted by the smooth, clean cork. When at last her fingers close around it, I can see how she's startled by the fit, although I am not, and by a balance she will soon understand.

I've seen that look before.

"That's right," I whisper, and I know that it is, even if I am so sorry to lose this, it's like something inside me is tearing. I know who would be proud; and if the image of the girl's eyes blur in mine, I still try to meet them for the moment it takes to manage, "Tomorrow. I will show you. Tomorrow."

I am a little better, walking back. I'm halfway to the dam before I realize that I'm not counting steps. It's possible that I will give up part of a place on water that has been only mine. But then, much of my life is empty enough. And since emptiness is also space, I may stop at Bud's desk in the morning.

I will thank him for thinking of me, and I will try to explain, about Edith's Rule.

lateral lines

Kate Small

My husband has a garage full of gear. I smell it in the dark. I wish I could hear the tired stories, about the old bamboo rod, bought by an uncle at a pawn shop in Rogue River, Oregon; about string and bacon, and a red-and-white bobber. Joe would spread his arms to indicate the vast, fat schools, hidden in inland ponds and creeks, places and fish as gone as he is.

"Eighteen-inch browns," he'd say, "eager to eat my dime-store flies."

The catalogs still come almost daily. I hold them to my chest and inhale the ink. He would read them in bed, sighing over glossy waders and bright reels. Joe died in a climbing accident on Mt. Shasta seven months ago, 62 days after we were married.

"Look," I hear Joe whisper in my sleep.

In my sleep, he shows me immaculate flies of rabbit and marabou on small sharp hooks. Every night, I dream of a fish I can't see, but whose shape and life I feel in my empty hands. I am 31 years old. Joe was barely 40.

You think it only happens on TV, but when someone dies, people do show up with quiches in Tupperware. Joe once told me that when he passed on, he wanted somebody to plug in a guitar and sing the Rolling Stones' "Between a Rock and a Hard Place." But I don't remember this until weeks after he is buried. I don't remember that he wanted everybody to dance in a bar. He wanted everybody to go outside and eat corn-on-the-cob and tomatoes.

After the funeral, a woman I've never met says, "You are lucky. You are young. There are other fish in the sea." She hands me a boxed coffee cake.

I go home and think about wedging myself into the broom closet, but at my kitchen sink is a petite Japanese-American woman, soaping dishes and sorting forks. In the midst of the casserole aftermath, my neighbor, Hiroko Yamate, has slipped in to rinse coffee cups and toss out the tuna surprise.

"I am a widow myself," Hiroko says, hovering agelessly between 40 and 60, "so I won't ask questions." When the fuss dies down, Hiroko keeps mowing my lawn. She puts my mail inside the door, and takes away the trash.

After a month, I go back to work. I write manuals, product specifications and instructions for a camera and film company in Portland, Oregon. I stare at my day's task: I am to write thoughts in speech balloons over the heads of people loading a new kind of film into a new kind of camera.

But Joe's most recent permits and camping reservations vibrate in my purse.

Joe's favorite river was the Grande Ronde, east of here, 200 miles long and flowing northeast until it crosses into Washington and enters the Snake River. Joe loved the lower part, the 28 miles accessible only by floating. There are still a very few native rainbows there, he said. He was to go with three friends at the end of November.

I look at my work. The stick people are smiling but their heads are too round, their eyes globular. There are blinding, white reflected spots near the pupils, minnows like bullets in long concrete tanks. I put my head on my desk. I think about how men talk about fishing—the music of their hands and bodies, the poetry of their lies. This big, that many.

"Remember when you winched that brute to shore?" I'd hear in my living room. Someone would pull out a photograph.

"Yep. His four-weight stopped it."

"Thing is, rust-colored nymphs outperform the gray, buddy."

Sometimes I would fall asleep listening to Joe's posse around my coffee table, around my onion dip and potato chips. I didn't want to learn its grammar, but I loved their foreign language.

I lift my head and call Joe's best friend. "I have Joe's permits," I say. "I want to go."

Joe's friends and I stand in a stream. We are ringed in white winter light and bare silver trees. We are held in the rich, filling quiet of pristine water, but something black and terrible is emanating from my chest. I am ruining their fishing.

Somebody catches something anyway. "The big guy grabs the fly!" Doug says.

"A sassy one," someone adds, but all the adrenaline that would make this fish-talk sing just isn't there. They try to tell a bright story about Joe, over sandwiches.

"A half-hour battle with 8-weight tackle," somebody says.

"A 200-yard dash," somebody else offers, but they are faking it for me, and their hearts are breaking. Gently, they release the two fish caught.

I tell Joe's friends I have to go home. "I'll pack out by myself," I say.

But they know I want to slip down into a stagnant pool. They know I want to climb below submerged deadfall and let swamp water close over my face. They stand, their bodies a cortege around me, their careful boot-steps on leaves a kind of holiness. Doug thinks he should talk while we walk, but to his credit he can't find a single word, and I am grateful.

I start packing Joe's things into boxes. Hiroko comes up from the kitchen and hands me a glass of orange juice. I am touching the place on the bed where Joe should be.

Hiroko takes Joe's pillow out of a garbage bag on the floor. "I'll keep this for you," she says.

I hope you don't know what it is like to put your hand in someone else's pocket for the first time, after you have lost him. I hope you have not felt the liveliness of a stick of gum, a guitar pick or a fisherman's shopping list.

"Turkey biots, brown hackle, white hackle," it says on the back of a receipt in his wallet. "Peacock herl, fine copper wire."

I walk in Joe's wool coat to the nearest water, a small dirty beach on the Willamette, Oregon's urban river. I pull his collar to me; I stare at shiploads of Toyotas in vast arid lots. At my feet are nails, condoms, ear plugs, and acres of broken glass.

"Glo Bug yarn, Krystal Flash, gray dubbing," it says in pencil on a gum wrapper in Joe's breast pocket.

I go home and open the garage. I pack Joe's old van. I drive to all the houses of his fishing friends, and parcel out his precious gear.

Three days later, I knock at their doors again and say I want it back. To a man, they arrange his things reverently on the seats of the van, as though tucking their first infant sons into bed. They hug me carefully—they think I might shatter.

"I need this," I say to Doug, when he hands me Joe's beloved Trident TL 906 F.

"You'll need a casting clinic," he says.

Y ou need a grief group," Hiroko says. She finds one and drives me to it. I am wearing Joe's patched cargo pants, I have lost too much weight, and my hair looks like a molting crayfish.

My nails are bitten away, but I extend my hand to Noleen, a hip-curvy, skin-glowing black woman of 29, a librarian with unnerving green eyes, a pile of sleek braids, and breasts recently gone to cancer.

"I lost a husband," I say.

"I'll never get one," Noleen says.

"Don't be too sure about that," Hiroko says.

"It'd take a damn rare husband," Noleen says. "Only the last of his species would want someone without these." She gestures to her own slim chest.

"You are," Hiroko says, "the sum of many other parts."

Everybody sits on folding chairs and itemizes their losses.

"What's your sob story?" Noleen asks Hiroko.

"I used to paint when my husband was living."

There is a silence like an empty canvas.

"I don't know if this is the right thing," I whisper.

"Okay," Hiroko sighs, "let's try fishing." It is 10 P.M.

"I'm coming with you," Noleen says. We drive to Lake Oswego, a suburb near Portland.

"Stop here," Hiroko says as we pass a vast golf course rolling into the black. "My husband used to play. There's a pond by the ninth hole."

It is midnight. We climb over a low fence, and no one stops us. I carry Joe's Trident in front of me, my eyes trained on the tip. Noleen holds her skirt away from the dew.

"Those are carp," Hiroko says of the huge flashing shapes moving over the bottom of the pool, "crossed with koi."

My fingers, my body and brain are numb, but I bait the only hook I have with beef jerky. I try candy corn, marshmallows, string cheese. I throw everything at those carp but my shoes and my sweater.

"I thought they'd be hungry," I say. There is ice forming on the pond.

"You can take a horse to water," Noleen says, "but you can't make anybody eat him."

I throw a golf ball, hard.

"We're going to have to learn how to do this," Hiroko sighs. Even though it is wet, we sit on the grass. There are no stars.

We sign up for a casting clinic.

"Precision matters," says Mark, the instructor. "Hitting what is a comparatively small window is crucial." There are 16 of us. Noleen, Hiroko and I are the only women. Mark reminds me of Joe: young, angular, obsessed—cut from the same water-loving, save-the-world cloth.

We line up to cast hookless pieces of yarn into a pool stocked with small trout, bluegills and carp. The fish are bored and wary, but something bulky takes a fancy to Noleen's jaunty red knot. String in tow, it speeds away.

"Wow," Hiroko says.

"Yes ma'am," one of our plaid-covered classmates says, "he's got some respectable muscular development there."

"How do you know he's not a she?" Noleen says, struggling. The linebacker fish darts away when her watch crystal catches the light.

"That," Mark the instructor says, "was just a carp."

"That," Noleen says, pinning him with her fierce green gaze, "was a big, strong fish."

Mark blushes. But I remember Joe saying, "Carp messes with a man's fly-fishing reputation."

It is my turn to cast. My arm chooses this moment to remember all the gutterballs I've ever thrown while bowling. I peer hopelessly at the water for Mark's crucial, comparatively small window. I cast, but I don't hit the water at all. Apparently my arm also remembers the bowling ball I once threw into an adjacent lane. I shut my eyes to summon Joe's musical laughter. Back here on earth, I see my male classmates wondering why I have equipment so in excess of my potential. Then they check out my car, Joe's rusty old Econoline van, and just like that, they get it, what has happened to me. Their shoulders melt, they are rooted to the spot. Their arms want to pat my back; they want to introduce me to their own kindly wives. They look at me apologetically.

"Maybe you need the 10-week intensive," Mark says to me.

Every Wednesday, Hiroko, Noleen and I meet at Grief Group, and then we go fishing at midnight on the golf course. Nobody bothers us. We don't catch anything, but Noleen, ever the librarian, researches carp.

"Carp," she says, "have adapted to every water system we have." Hiroko stands far away from me, to avoid my less predictable casting efforts. "Carp," Noleen says, "have maintained their numbers amidst all forms of harvesting: commercial netting, bow-hunting, angling." She ducks.

"No threat to their numbers here," Hiroko says, liberating my hook from a tree.

Now these," Mark says at our next class, "are your classic trout bugs, your true flies: mayflies, stoneflies, midges and caddisflies." He holds a tiny hooked puff under Hiroko's nose, but he's staring at the silver chain around Noleen's dark neck, at her coffee-smooth skin.

"How's a fish going to see that?" Hiroko asks, peering at the fly.

"A midge nymph may be less than one-eighth-inch long," Mark says, coming to.

"I thought Midge was Barbie's best friend," I say.

"A tomboy," Hiroko nods. "Competition for Ken."

"Doesn't anybody dig for worms any more?" Noleen says.

"That's in the cartoons," Mark says, "and that's bait."

Drum? Gar? Are these fish? I ask the ceiling, pulling up from a sweaty, Joe-filled, Joe-absent dream. We are not supposed to be able to enter the same river twice, but night after night I founder in place, and the water is much too hot.

I get up to look at the photo of Joe in my wallet. He cradles a huge, gorgeous steelhead, nearly kissing it. As though it might swim into the embrace of his grin, his eyes crinkled in the too-bright sun, his cheeks and forehead burned red. The belly of his lip is as smooth and pink as a baby's—I can nearly taste it. This picture is unbearable.

In February, I ask Mark if we should sign up for the next session: Intermediate Casting.

"How about taking the beginning class again?" he says, gently. "And how about buying a more appropriate rod?"

"Well, I don't care what you say," Noleen says, smacking Mark with her Orvis catalog. "I'm getting the Silver Label 906 4. It packs down small, and it matches my jewelry."

But I purchase my first, own, fishing gear.

Just when Noleen, Hiroko and I are beginning to smell spring, something changes in our secret golf-course pond. One bright night, the water is nervous, tails smash around.

"You go first," Noleen says.

I cast. My new reel starts shrieking, and because I have never heard this before, so do I.

"Shhhh!" Noleen hisses.

There is a glimpse of fin, and I yank blindly. The clamor of my heart in my throat makes me afraid: Is this what Joe's heart did when he died? But I hear Joe say what he says in my dreams: "This is how hell breaks loose, and it is beautiful."

I run and slip. I hear myself laughing. The fish gets away, but somehow, it is my first fish.

At the next clinic, I try to describe the giant fish with whiskers, and teeth.

"Fangs," I say.

"THIS frigging big," Noleen says, helpfully.

"What did you use?" someone asks.

"Turkey sandwich," I say.

"And there were a thousand tails waving above the surface," Hiroko says.

"A thousand?" Mark asks.

"A lot," Noleen says.

"Grass carp are usually planted to control weed growth," Mark says.

"Grass carp," Noleen says, "originated in eastern China and Russia, and are citizens of the world."

"Eventually, you're going to get arrested for fishing on private property," Mark says.

I start wearing Joe's fly vest. After work, I practice casting at the dirty beach on the Willamette, by myself. But sometimes I find myself staring into an open fly box, at Joe's dry, perfect flies.

At night, I want to pierce my hand with one. I envy Joe's intimacy with all the fish he ever caught. Let me be their blood-sister then, I say in my sleep.

Noleen signs the three of us up for Mark's fly-tying class without asking first.

"What the hell . . . . " Hiroko says, so we go.

Now," Mark says. "When a grasshopper lands on a pond, it tries to kick itself free. Use sharp little jerks to copy this motion."

"Of course carp," Noleen interrupts, "can feel the shadow made by a fly line in the air."

"Usually," Mark says, trying to ignore her, "the hopper's thrashing just gets him in deeper and he drowns. Float the fly quietly, and copy that."

"Often," Noleen breaks in, "a carp that bypasses a thrashing bug will surface to snack on a water-logged one." She nods.

"Look," he says, turning to her. "Carp are trash fish." He's doomed.

"That's racist," she says, standing up.

"Carp are weeds," he says. He gazes at her helplessly. I watch the left-to-right motion of his eyes as he traces her broad forehead, her arched brows, her high cheeks.

"Carp are immigrants!" she says.

"Like us," he says, slowly, thinking.

"Hey," Hiroko nudges me, "he's falling for her."

"To pieces," I say, "and she doesn't even know."

"Listen up, pool boy," Noleen declares. "Carp can live in inner-city water."

"So can I," Mark says softly, but she's just getting started.

"Carp," Noleen says, "can live in water that spontaneously combusts and glows in the dark!"

"Yes," Mark says, "and carp can see quite well. They can see your fly, and they can see you. So you need to learn how to tie good ones." He looks at the giant clump of feathers she's glued to a cork.

"That's the worst one I ever saw," I whisper to Hiroko.

"Worked on him," she says.

A t our next-to-last casting clinic, Hiroko hooks and pulls in a small hatchery trout. Everybody claps, because, apparently, any trout is better than a carp.

"Now that's white bread," says Noleen, shaking her head.

But Hiroko holds the fish gently, then brings it close to her face. She is reading its shifts in hue. She is memorizing its lines, its architecture, the armature of its interior sculpture.

Noleen and I gather to her. The fish has old holes, healed in its mouth, and old hardware hanging from one of them. Mark unhooks him, and Hiroko drops him back to the deep. He flies down to the dark of his not-home water.

I retrieve Joe's pillow from Hiroko's garage. I start making flies from the soft white down.

A lthough Noleen has been tying better, if flamboyant, flies, she has stopped casting.

"I don't want to catch one," she says. "I keep seeing the scars in their mouths." I try not to look at the straight plane of her shirt. My eyes fall instead on her Hare's Ear Nymph, neatly bound with gold oval tinsel. I smile. It is in miniature the hat of a strong, proud woman singing in a church pew.

Hiroko has begun painting. She gives Mark an extraordinary watercolor of a carp, its body twisted in such a way that you can see how the olive-and-bronze back transitions to a yellow-and-cream belly.

"It is beautiful," Mark murmurs. He holds the paper like it is the creature itself.

I look over his shoulder. There is impossible brevity in the brush strokes, yet the muscle and wit of the animal seem to burst from the page.

"Carp . . . " Mark says.

"Are important in the culture to which I was born," Hiroko says firmly. "Now," she adds, "quit treading water and go catch that one," she points at Noleen.

I buy a small green box for my Joe's-Pillow flies. I cast them on my dirty neighborhood Willamette. I see that their soft, full wings allow them to land gently. They imitate nothing in particular, but the fish cluster up and kiss them, curious. I let out a breath. I am casting well.

In March we get arrested at the golf-course for trespassing. Hiroko calls Mark on her cell phone to bail us out. "I was tired of the ninth hole anyway," Noleen says.

"And Grief Group," I say.

"We're ready for wilder water," Hiroko says.

"The Grande Ronde," I say.

"Your van was impounded," Mark says, driving us home.

At our next tying class, he takes a new tack.

"Carp, as some of you like to point out, are smart. They won't chase a second-rate fly. They certainly won't sucker for anything as obvious," here Mark looks at me, "as a turkey sandwich. They're wily, they strike hard, they slam and run for an excellent tussle. Carp, I must conclude, require skill. But what I want you to think about is, how and why wild is in all ways superior to hatchery made . . . . "

"Of course many of us," Noleen interjects, "were spawned in cement boxes."

"And carp are not from hatcheries," Hiroko says.

"True," Mark says, putting up his hand. "But, I'm just asking you to consider whether they're sucking resources away from other, more fragile fish. Besides," he adds, "they're awfully bony."

"Who are you calling bony?" Noleen mutters. Over in the casting pond, there's a riot in the shallows. "Carp spawning sure is a splashy affair," I say.

"No kidding," Hiroko says.

By April, the stick people in the tech manuals at work begin to look like they want to be fishing. There they are, dehydrated and trapped in empty white space, earnestly inserting their film into cameras. But secretly, they are thinking about the mysteries of reading the water. Secretly, they are thirsty for the big, wet deep.

I leave early. At three o'clock a hatch is just coming off, and my stretch of the Willamette is broken by gappy mouths. Scrap iron decays on the sand around me. Styrofoam doesn't decay. Three bleach bottles and a man's leather dress shoe lap in the waves at my thighs. But even here, the undulation beneath the emerging caddis is as big and lazy as the moon, and I am filled with stillness. Even here, I am surprised by the fine slowness of fishing, as arresting as midnight snowfall in a city.

With the stuff of Joe's pillow, I pull in a four-pound fish, the first I have brought to shore.

We consider each other.

"Look," I say to Joe.

But I am not going to tell you what kind of fish he was. Because suppose he was a fine little native. We can't afford to take him as an indication of a river's recovery; nor the sign of a true species thriving in what is functionally a sewer, and a big wet road. No; better to think of that fish as a miracle.

Maybe I should propose that he was a carp. My husband was a spring-creek fisherman of grace and finesse, and a passionate advocate of endangered, aboriginal fish. But maybe he was wrong about carp. A good carp, I believe, has the power to do two things: to take you back to that first, thrilling childhood catch; and to force you to look for the beauty in the hell that is surely breaking loose all around us. If there are trash fish, we made them. We are the weeds. Perhaps we should feel admiration as well as fear for the creatures who eke out a living where we allow sawmills to creep into our home rivers. Joe's death has taught me this: There isn't time to waste. We are no longer nested in a slow geologic tempo. It has taken us less than 200 years to wreck what it took millions of years to make. I wish you true fly water, I really do, but fish when and where you can. Fish in the rain and put your permit in a Ziploc. Cast into the heart of the mud. And if you do catch a big, smart, hard-fighting carp—where their numbers are good and they are not made poisonous—I suggest that you thank him for the ride, say a prayer to the universe, and take that fish home and eat him. Yes, he will be bony, but you will be obliged to chew more slowly. You will be obliged to taste the animal will in your food. That is a gift.

I let my Willamette fish go. And with that catch-and-release I am hooked. Something—Joe's obsession—has rooted in my soft sediment. I have taken to seeing any water's surface, crinkling with flying ants, as an opportunity, for hunting, and for witness.

In May, on Joe's bright, quick Grande Ronde river, my friends and I discover that it is nice to fish freely in daylight. The fish sip up, sunbathing.

"Carp," Noleen reads from a library book, "possess a lateral line, a series of nerve endings used to detect low-frequency vibrations."

Even I am sick of hearing about carp. I squint at the fish I really want, moving into deeper water.

Hiroko sits on a rock and sketches in ink, a perfect beetle, just blundered into the drink. She tears off the page, frowning. I wade back and grab it. Somehow she has nailed it: You can tell the bug isn't struggling, as much as it is trying to walk slowly back to land across the film. I am awed.

"But the water isn't right," she shrugs.

I go back to my rod. "I'm the only one fishing," I say over my shoulder.

"No you're not," they both say back.

For half an hour of happy quiet, I try to cast my way out of a knot problem.

Hiroko speaks up, "Sometimes you just have to cut and start over."

"Lateral lines," Noleen reads out loud, "help a carp remain in close contact with its school- or shoalmates."

When the sun hits the gold zone, we steam six ears of corn in a camping pot and slice three Roma tomatoes. We unwrap huge turkey sandwiches and squeeze anchovy paste onto crackers.

"Between a rock and a hard place!" I belt out at the river.

Suddenly there comes a flotilla of small yellow-bodied insects with white, uplifted wings. I don't tell Hiroko and Noleen that this is Joe's funeral we are having—they know. We are schooling.

When we graduate from fly-tying class, Mark presents us with computer-printed certificates. Everyone exchanges phone numbers.

As we head for the parking lot, Hiroko gives us each a small black-and-white etching of three of my best Joe's-Pillow flies. How I wish he could see mine.

"Excuse me," Mark says to Hiroko and me. He follows Noleen to her car.

"I tied this for you," he says to her. "If you cast gently, it hangs vertically, the same way the tuft supports a thistle seed." He places it very carefully on the flat pink of her palm.

Hiroko and I amble past and pretend not to listen. "And this," he says (he is still holding her fingers). "I hope it matches the spring mulberry fall along the bottomland creek I am going to show you."

For the first time that I can think of, Noleen is speechless.

This makes me smile for three days. Then I think of the woman at Joe's funeral who said, "You are lucky. You are young. There are other fish in the sea." She might be right. But I believe this:

There is an unfixable wound made in our earth's skin when people like Joe die young—they are too rare. Joe held a spot, he maintained a balance in the terrestrial sphere, like the one perfect cutthroat you saw once, one of a remnant population in a tiny rivulet. Joe was as original as the breathtaking spotted natives hanging on in interior drainages. He was pure, and endemic to the isolated brooks and spring holes of his own childhood. In him, we have lost one fine custodian of the natural world. His places and their fish are going away. It will take many good men and women to savor, and save, them.

In the meantime, my nights have softened: I see Joe in wild places and hard-to-reach headwaters. I deed him Arctic coasts and isolated ranges and fish as sweet as my own skin. Tomorrow, late afternoon will blow cottonwood into the water. There he is, at the downwind side of a lake, dusty with seeds. The surface trembles with emerging duns. There will be a giant bend to the rod and Joe's laughter in the chase. In my sleep, there is enough. Enough thistle, dandelion, cattail, and spotted browns. There is enough for Joe, for the fish, for me. In the undertow of dreams, I no longer separate the rare fish from the rare man; his hands and catch run together in my arms. I am a fly fisherman now, and he follows me, hiding where the trees and brush lean out. We school. I feel and find him in the lateral lines of sleep.

For Eli, who was a wild thing.

opening day

Richard Chiappone

S he's more or less moved in with him," Dave said. From the minute we'd met at the floatplane dock in King Salmon he'd been trying to tell me about his wife Mary and what she had going with some guy from her night school class. I wasn't having any part of it. Dave looked terrible, shot, ruined—even I could see that—but after a whole winter working on the North Slope I was not giving up the first week of trout season to somebody else's misery.

I pretended to be looking for something in the side pocket of one of my travel bags. "Dave," I said, without looking at him, "come on. It's opening day."

I know that sounds cold-blooded, because Dave and I go way back—to the pipeline days and the boom years in Anchorage—but part of the beauty of fishing is that it's something you can do with a friend year after year and never have to know any more about him than this: Does he prefer to fish upstream or down? Streamers or nymphs? How good does he need the camp cooking to be and what does he drink and how much? It had been a very long winter and I didn't want to think about anything for the next week, except the river and the fish.

I climbed into the Cessna and buckled myself in. All the way out to Katmai I could feel Dave brooding in the seat behind me. I was glad we couldn't talk over the engine noise.

At the Katmai Visitor Center a young woman in a Smokey Bear hat read us the park rules. As always: Keep fifty yards away from any bear, a hundred yards away from a sow with cubs. Store food in the log caches in the campground. No food on your person while on the river. No fish in possession. If you have a fish on and a bear enters the area, BREAK THE FISH OFF!

They always delivered that last part with wide eyes. I think the Park Service has them rehearse for it.

"It's too early in the year for most of the bears." She seemed to be apologizing. "Still, it pays to be careful."

Yes, it pays to be careful. I looked at Dave to see if that registered with him, but he just stared at his toes, really miserable now that it was clear I didn't want to hear about his wife's affair.

We got our permits and hauled our gear to the nearly empty campground. After the tent was pitched and the food stored in the cache, I put my waders on and rigged my fly rod. I had my vest packed with fly boxes and my trout net snapped to my belt. I was ready to go. Dave and I hadn't shared a dozen words since we'd landed.

Dave sat on the edge of the picnic table and strung his rod. His hands trembled as he threaded the line, and after he finished he saw that he had missed one of the guides and had to do it over again. He looked so bad I almost asked him to tell me about Mary.

Instead, I went to the cache for the single-malt Scotch that Dave had found a taste for working the offshore rigs in the North Sea. It was our regular opening-day drink and just about the only ritual we allowed ourselves. I put two tin cups on the picnic table and poured. I sat on the table beside him.

We sat there in silence a while, sipping our drinks and watching the clouds build over the lake as the evening wind rolled in from Bristol Bay, 40 miles to the west. Somewhere back in the woods an owl hooted and a woodpecker hammered away. I finished my drink and set the cup down with a clank, but Dave made no move to get going. We sat a bit longer, still not saying anything.

Up in Prudhoe Bay on the Slope we work all winter because the ground is frozen then, and the trucks and drilling equipment can move across the permafrost. We work 12-hour days, although words like day and night have little meaning in 24-hour darkness. We work seven days a week because there is no point in having time off in a work camp without alcohol or women. We work a month at a stretch, sometimes longer. And through it all, through the darkness, the boredom, the almost unbelievable cold, trout season is what I dream about. Opening day was supposed to be a good thing, maybe the best day of the whole year. I hadn't figured on Dave packing this trouble along.

I poured myself another drink and held it under my nose. I love the smoky, peaty smell of Scotch, and the smell of neoprene waders, the smell of the lake and the spruce forest and last year's rotting cottonwood leaves. I was sure that once we got fishing Dave would be all right. But Dave wasn't moving.

Out over the lake, an osprey began to hover, wings cupped, scooping air up under its body, furiously holding itself in place against the wind as it zeroed in on its target.

"Somebody's ready to fish," I said. Dave looked up as the bird folded its wings and dropped like a missile. At the last second it swooped flat and punched through the surface with its talons. It came up with a small trout and flapped off around the point.

When the bird was gone Dave said, "I worked with a guy in Wyoming once, back when I was still running pipe." He said it calmly, off-handedly, like it was an interesting little story anybody might tell in camp.

"It was winter. Cold and windy with no trees to slow it down. This guy was sitting in the company pickup, running the heater, when a cable on the big crane snapped. I'd never heard of that before, a cable breaking. I'm talking about steel braid. But it broke, and the hook ball was directly over the truck when it let go. Came down about the speed of that osprey there."

I stared out at the rings on the lake where the bird had pulled the fish out. Something in Dave's tone told me this wasn't just a work story, but I nodded and he continued.

"The guy was just stepping out of the rig—no idea any of this is happening right over his head—when the ball went through the roof of the cab. Blew the windows and windshield out, went straight through the floor and into the ground under the truck. He never got a scratch, but he was shaking so bad they gave him the rest of the day off."

"Good outfit," I said, trying to lighten things up a bit. Dave went straight on with it. No sign of a smile.

"When he got home, there was a strange truck in his drive. His wife was a teacher and should've been at school. He figured burglars, so he took his bird gun from the window rack and let himself in with his key, real quiet like. He was feeling pretty lucky after that crane thing. Who wouldn't? Seems the furnace had gone out at the school and they'd sent everybody home. Kids, teachers, everybody. This guy's wife caught a ride with the principal." Dave did laugh then, though there was no humor in it. " 'Caught a ride,' that's funny. She was catching a ride all right. You can pretty much guess what the guy walked in on."

Dave took a sip. I thought there was more to the story, but he was quiet again. He sat hunched over his knees, holding his cup in both hands. Except for the fly rod across his lap he looked like the hard-timers you see in the prison movies.

Then I said it. "Who's the guy?"

"Just some guy in Wyoming," Dave said.

"No, I mean Mary's new friend."

He gave me a glance, maybe checking to see if I really wanted to get into this after being such a prick about it all day. I looked out over the lake as if it didn't matter to me one way or the other. But it did now. It mattered, and I guess I knew it had all along.

"She met him at night school."

"So you said."

"His name is Lance."

"Aw, Dave," I said. "Lance?"

It poured out of him then.

"I found them in the bathtub. That's the part that got me." He ran one hand through his hair. "The tub!" he said. "I mean, falling into bed can happen, you know? It's so fast. You get talking to somebody nice. You share a drink, maybe a couple. Next thing you know. . . . " He left that unfinished.

"It can happen," I agreed.

"But a bath? You've got to take some time to run a bath." Dave stared down at the streamer he had hanging from the hook keeper on his rod. He looked at it like he had no idea in the world how it had gotten knotted on his line like that. "They had bubbles," he said, miserably.

"Anybody get hurt?"

"Just her car. The Subaru."

"I remember the Subaru. Piece of shit."

"Is now," he said. "I took a nail set and a hammer and punched about a half a million holes in it. Worked on it for an hour. Could've smashed it to bits, but I just didn't have the energy for the big noisy stuff. God, it looked funny though. You could strain macaroni through it. Later some furniture got broken, a couple other things."

I said, "You okay now?"

"Popsicles," Dave said. "Popsicles are my salvation."

I felt the Scotch warming my cheeks a bit and wondered if I'd heard that right. It was pretty clear that Dave wasn't going to fish until he told me every detail of this. I said, "Are we still having the same conversation?"

"Anger management. It's the latest. Seems it's okay to be pissed, but not to beat anybody up over it. Ask my therapist."

"Your therapist." I pictured those rainbows out there scarfing up sock-eye smolts while we sat in camp talking therapy.

"I'm getting a little help," Dave said. He didn't seem at all embarrassed to admit that. "Every time I feel like smashing something, I'm supposed to have a popsicle. Deflects the energy or something."

Dave in therapy. It had come to that. I wondered what that would be like. A therapist. My therapist. What kinds of things would I say to somebody like that?

"Popsicles," I said. "It works?"

"Got a house full of guns and haven't killed anybody yet."

"That's one for the plus column all right."

He managed half a smile at that. Then a shadow passed across his face again.

"Mary's outgrown me. That's what they call it. Like I'm old skin or something. She's moving on, becoming."

"Becoming what?"

"Just becoming. They do that now. They become. She thinks I'm Fred Flintstone," he said. "But I'm not. I am not Fred Flintstone."

This was all new to me. Therapists. Popsicles. Back when I got divorced we just hurled blame around, called each other names. It seemed to work as well as anything.

I'd heard enough to think about, but Dave was not done yet.

"I swear, she used to appreciate some things about me. The way I could fix stuff around the house, build stuff. You know the way I am. I have to believe she used to admire me for that." He tipped his head back and squinted up into the canopy of the big cottonwoods overhead. When he spoke again his voice was one long sigh. "She should have hired me, not married me."

I wished I could disagree with that. I got the feeling this was the moment when I was supposed to offer some sort of insight, but I was drawing a horrible blank.

I said, "Dave, you think you can fish now?"

Dave was very quiet again as we walked upriver to a series of pools and pocket water right out of a travel brochure. We would fish our way back down to the campground, taking advantage of the all-night solstice light. There wold be plenty of time to make up the lost sleep next winter.

It was late, and we had the river to ourselves. The spruce forest was throwing long shadows across the cutbank pools on the far side. Though no fish were rising, everything else about the night whispered trout. Dave waded in and began beating the water with casts sloppy even by Alaskan standards. It seemed like a poor way to start a trip. He thrashed his way around a bend downstream and out of sight.

Should I have said something more to him? Talked it through for the rest of the night? The rest of the trip maybe? I tried to imagine him sitting alone in his house in Fairbanks with a freezer full of popsicles. What was there to say to that?

I let the water rest a bit, then started fishing the pools he had rushed through. When I caught up with him half an hour later, he was standing almost mid-river, holding his rod high over his head and palming the reel against the surge of a very heavy fish heading downstream below him. As I waded up, the trout cut out of the main current and shot into a slough to the right of us. It broke water there, twisting across the surface in a frantic arc. Whatever else I'd had on my mind was gone. We were just fishing now. Finally.

"Nice," I said over the rush of the knee-deep water.

Dave grunted. He put more pressure on the reel, and the fish rolled again.

That's when we saw the bears.

I saw the sow first, on the bank to our left, less than 20 yards away, about three good leaps for a grizzly. She hauled herself up out of the high grass onto her hind legs, craning her neck to take in the commotion. Her honey-blond fur rippled in the wind as she shifted her weight from paw to paw and stretched her neck to sniff the air. I didn't see the cub until it walked out into the shallows in front of her. It was a three-year-old, nearly as large as its mother. They both strained to see what was going on in the slough where the trout splashed wildly again. They were looking right through us. I felt every hair on my body stand up and start vibrating.

I grabbed Dave by the back of his fly vest. "Break it off!"

"No chance," he said. He cranked the reel and reared back harder on the rod, trying to turn the fish out into the current again. The sow stepped down into the river next to the cub and I felt a current of fear run down my back.

I reminded myself that this was a national park, that these bears had been around humans all their lives, that the rangers had clever names for them: Diver, Scarface, Saddleback. But I found myself thinking about a man in Anchorage who had stumbled into a grizzly while berry picking in the hills above town the summer before. The bear clamped its jaws on the man's face and swung him around like a rag before discarding him. A month after the attack I saw him in the Safeway, his face crisscrossed with stitches and wires, one eye covered with a patch, one ear gone. His cheek bones had been so thoroughly crushed that they had to wire his jaw to his forehead. The bear's teeth had punctured his skull and brain and left him without a sense of taste or smell.

I was suddenly furious with Dave. I had troubles too, personal problems. Who didn't? Did I put my friends in the path of an ugly death because of them?

I tugged on his elbow. "Let's get the hell out of here."

Dave pulled away from me and started down the middle of the river, walking directly in front of the bears as he applied lateral pressure with the rod and finally horsed the fish back out into the current. He went on wading downstream, the trout ahead of him in the river once again like a dog on a leash. The bears watched him pass. They looked at him and then at me and back at him again—as though choosing, I thought. Then they turned and disappeared into the willows behind them.

When they were gone, I walked to shore and stood there until the muscles in my thighs stopped quivering. Then I went looking for Dave.

This time I found him on a gravel bar a hundred yards down river. He was still working the trout. I expected some outward sign of near death to show on his face, but he was intent on the fish, calmly giving it a little line when it wanted to run, picking it back up again when he was able, until he had it in the shallows.

"Dave," I said. "Have you gone nuts? You know you're going to release it anyway."

"I'd just like it to be my choice," he said. "My idea."

He reached to unhook the fly, but the trout spotted him and went berserk the way hooked fish do sometimes when they put a face on what it is that's tormenting them. It exploded in a strong run that took it into a very deep hole and under a downed tree there. Dave was right behind it, wading in up to his knees, then to his hips, and deeper yet, until the water was nearly at the top of his waders.

He balanced there at the edge of the drop off, elbows flared birdlike to keep them up out of the river, hanging on as if that was the most important thing in the world, as if he was the first person this ever happened to.

It was a scene from a winter dream, the kind I have in the middle of the endless darkness and cold up at Prudhoe Bay when, at the end of a shift, I lie in my bunk and close my eyes and this is what I see: I see a man standing in a river, rod deeply bowed against a very big fish, the surface of the river almost black in the shadow of the far bank. Above the man there is the jagged sawtooth silhouette of the spruce forest, black against the summer night sky; and, higher yet, a pair of eagles, motionless on the thermals over the lake.

But this was not a dream. This was what I'd waited for all winter, what I'd worked for. A beautiful river. A big fish. An old friend to share them with. It should have been everything I could ever want. Yet in the middle of it I imagined walking down a narrow hallway in a cold house, the weak winter sun the only light as I pressed my face against a hollow wooden door and listened to the soft and familiar female laughter on the other side. God, is there anything you can really feel that you haven't lived on your own?

Dave's rod straightened and the line fell slack across the surface of the hole. He turned and waded slowly back toward me, reeling in as he came ashore in that stooped-over, fished-out posture that usually indicated the end of a very long and hard trip. He was looking at me as if I might offer him something.

"Maybe I should have done things differently," he said. He stood there waiting for my answer, but I had nothing for him. Not even a popsicle.

"Come on," I said, turning away. "Let's go back up and work the water that fish dragged you through."

"Wait," Dave said. "I mean it now. Tell me what I should have done." Dave was looking at me crazy-eyed, like I might really have some answer for him, and it was clear that it both gave him hope and scared him at the same time. "Tell me," he said. "What would you do?"

I'm no philosopher. Not even a therapist. So, can somebody explain to me how 15 years of friendship comes down to two guys up to their knees in maybe the most beautiful river in the world with nothing but clear, empty water connecting them in any real way?

I didn't think so.

I said, "Dave, sometimes you just lose them."

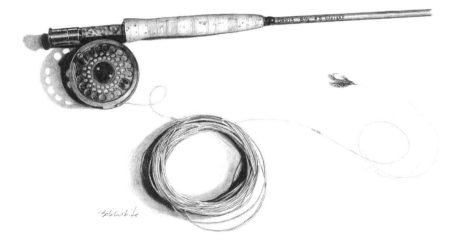

autumn hope

Keith McCafferty

By the time the steelhead arrive, it is late in the fall. The sockeyes that brought the grizzlies to the bank are skeletons on the cobbles. The leaves have turned from red to brown and the sky from blue to gray.

Some prefer it this way. It clears the banks of fishermen who want to spend a pleasant afternoon. It leaves the river for those who favor the company of eagles over the brotherhood of men, who enjoy the burn of blood returning to frozen toes, and who are best suited to endure those long stretches of silence that are the hallmark of the sport.

The man who struggles into his waders is a dreamer, as are most who seek fish that live more vividly in the imagination than at the bend of a hook. He is 50 this season, a heart-attack survivor, a businessman of no particular consequence, a husband, a father of two. He is old enough to remember years when the run came earlier, before commercial fishing eradicated steelhead with the genetic impulse, or the gall, to return to the river in the company of cannery-bound salmon. He balls his hands into fists inside fingerless gloves and crosses his arms against his chest for warmth.

A snow squall passed through the canyon yesterday. Snow was still falling when he bought his license in a whistle-stop town along the Canadian National Rail Line 30 miles downriver, saddle-sore and bleary-eyed after a 15-hour drive from his home in Oregon. It was falling again that evening while he fished, glancing up to spot a bald eagle perched in a yellow pine tree across the river, its head the one white dot that never moved. The snow melted from the riverbanks overnight and now, in the clear early morning, it dusts the escarpments above the river, its purity in stark contrast to the dreary tan of the lower slopes.

He steps into the river, pulling line from the reel. Tall and sparely built, he fishes a 15-foot rod and bends forward as he leads the fly line downstream. From a distance he looks to be as intent on his fishing as the heron that spears silver fingerlings on the rocks in the shallows, and in fact the two share a poised, predatory bearing that, in past seasons, has served both very well. Most who come here cannot summon either the man's or the heron's concentration and that is one reason they are the better fishermen, although on this river the definition is relative. Nobody goes steelhead fishing here to catch steelhead. If you only want to feel the rod bend, you go to rivers that flood with hatchery fish in winter. You troll your hotshot in the scribbled gasoline wake of the boat in front of you, adding your exhaust to the one that follows.

You come here to get away from that. Sometimes, the man thinks, you come here to get away from everything.

At the bottom of the run he wades out and sits down on a rock. Another angler approaches from a bend downriver, tapping his wading staff in front of him like a blind man crossing a street. He stops nearby and tips his brimmed felt hat, a gesture as uncommon on a steelhead river as it is anywhere.

The tall man glances up. "Every time I drive here," he says, "I tell myself it's going to be the last time. The river's not worth it, eh? But then I come back." Although not Canadian, he subconsciously affects both the speech patterns and laid-back manner the moment he crosses the border. All his life, it seems to him, he has adapted to others around him, but only recently has he come to count the cost. He defines the lines in his cheeks with a thin smile.

Like most of his acquaintances on this river, he has never offered his name to a fellow fisherman. Instead, the two men exchange the names of the flies they fish—Purple Peril, Silver Hilton, Lady Caroline. The newcomer displays a Spey pattern tied with the soft hackles from the

rump of a ringneck pheasant. The tall man allows that he once caught a fish on a similar pattern, one with a little more red in it.

He rises on his long legs, cinches up his wader belt. "Better get back at it. That's the secret," he says, and strides back toward the top of the run.

But only a few casts into his second pass, while negotiating a rock garden where the current divides into sinewy ropes, he feels a pressure building behind his eyes. He reels up and rubs a hand under his sunglasses, then wipes it on his waders. Tears on a steelhead river, a man of his age. What am I coming to? he thinks. He looks absently into his fly box, but can find nothing that inspires his confidence. He catches himself drifting again, his eyes welling for no reason he can fathom, just as they have at home, and shakes his head to clear it. He was up at five this morning to be first on the water and suddenly he is so tired he can barely make it up the bank. Crossing the railroad tracks to his truck, he leans the rod against the camper shell, then musters the last of his energy to drag a pad and a couple blankets under the last leaves of an aspen.

Maybe it's only exhaustion, he tells himself. If I can just rest for a while it will pass.

When he opens his eyes a half hour later, a cluster of bighorn ewes are pointing their cloven hooves at him. A lone ram backs up a foot and tilts his head to peer over the curl of his horn. The sheep are tame here, coming down out of the granite to graze on the riverbank nearly every day. They regard the man with a respectful, distanced interest that reminds him of the way people look at him after he has been in the city too long, when the voices that compete for dominance in his head grow too distracting. He used to fool everyone all the time. Now they give him that same sidelong glance.

"What are you looking at?" he says.

The sheep prick their ears, but they are still standing there after he has tossed his blankets into the truck and driven away.

When he had left Portland, his wife had walked out to the truck with him. "I don't understand why you have to go," she'd said. It was what she told him every time he went on a trip, and for her they were the words spoken to make him say he loved her.

In fact, he wasn't sure why he was going. It wasn't just to catch a steelhead, nor had it been for some years now. Part of the reason was

just to get out of the house, away from his job and the wolves of credi-
tors who never seemed to camp too far from the door. He understood
that. But gradually he had been losing touch with himself, and what
worried him was how easy it was to accept. He knew the skin that
had drawn over his senses was a natural process of aging. It was like
a shell with which he blunted the pressures of life. But as the pulse
underneath became increasingly hard to hear, matters of decision had
grown more difficult. Life had begun to turn hazy. Lately, he'd had a
hard time focusing on the people around him, even on the woman he
had lived with for almost thirty years.

If he had paused to think about it, he might have realized he was
taking this trip in spite of himself. He was heading north to reclaim some
immediacy to his life, some return of the wonder that his own defenses
have acted to erase, some sense of his identity. He was going by instinct
and he was a little bit scared.

About a mile upriver from the bank where the sheep graze there is
a deep run marked by an enormous copper-colored boulder. It is two
bends above a feeder stream that pulls in half the annual run, across the
railroad tracks and down a steep hill. There aren't a lot of fish to fish
for. But it's a long walk and a long way from anyone else, which to him
is all that is important.

When he was younger he used to tell people that he fished alone for
reasons of the soul, but those were nothing but words. Later, he said that
he came to the river to be alone with his thoughts. That may have been
closer to the truth, but perspective changes the more deeply one becomes
immersed in the transactions of civilized living, when with one of those
rare insights of age you suddenly understand what Thoreau really meant
when he wrote about men leading lives of quiet desperation. The last few
times he had gone to the river, he had tried not to think at all.

The thing about fishing, he'd come to realize, was that it gave a man
hope, and each cast built a little more of it. If he could sufficiently lose
himself to the hope, whether or not it was justified by the strike of a
steelhead, then the everyday concerns that occupied his mind, that wind
of voices competing for his attention, would lose its power for a time.

He knew that the wind would come back, of course. But that was two
days down the road, maybe four. When you're an adult, caught in the
whirl of the clock, four days out of the wind is a long time.

When he parks the truck, the wind is blowing down from the north in sharp gusts, rattling the leaves and driving them against the rails of the train track. He zips a rain jacket over his cable-knit sweater and jams a wool watch cap over his ears. His nose is running as he hikes along the twisted path that leads to the river.

The run is as he remembers, a current that quickens the step when he hears it. Then he rounds an upstream bend and sees the river plane away below into a sweeping narrow darkness.

Stopping at the top of the run, he consults his fly box. This time a pattern called Autumn Hope catches his eye. It is a fly of his own design. He turned it out at his vise the night before he left the city—silver body, a deep purple wing, two turns of soft black hackle at the collar. He ties it on, squints at it, drops it into the water, watches the feathers breathe.

"I'd eat it," he says out loud, and begins to work out line.

Stepping into deeper water, he feels something squish under the hobnails on his boots. Gaseous bubbles burst through the surface and he is overwhelmed with a nauseating stench. A rotting salmon dislodges from a crevice in the rocks. It drifts away, rolling over and over, disks of decay peering up whitely through the water like dreaming eyes. This is not a river for a fisherman with a weak stomach.

Nor is it a promising note on which to start the afternoon. But then something has changed; the trigger of scent has alerted him to a subtle shift in his environment and for a moment he can't put a finger on it. He shivers involuntarily, craning his head to search for movement in the willows. Only three weeks before, grizzly bears had walked these banks. They had followed the pinks up the feeders into the hills, but where they left tracks the magnetic alignment of the earth seems to be disturbed, and now that he is alone on the river he can feel the attraction and repulsion of the tumbling poles. He feels the wind sift through the hairs on his neck. He's not scared so much as alert in a way he hasn't been in a very long time.

Beginning to fish, he discovers a cadence to his casting that eluded him yesterday. Double-handed rods demand precise timing, but the reward is a form of dance, a rip and swish of line that is very much an end in itself. This is not an inconsiderable bonus on a river where the fisherman is so rarely interrupted by the fish, and he surrenders to the motion, the rocking rhythm floating him far away. A better angler does not allow himself to be so easily lost—his heart is swimming with the fly, where it's supposed to be. But the rod holds out its hand and he is too much of a romantic to ignore the invitation.

The afternoon passes without his really being aware. The rhythm of casting becomes internalized so that his focus returns to the river below him, where Autumn Hope searches current threads for fish that he envisions as mysteriously glowing, each a lantern to the next as they make their way upriver. The sun draws its arc and catches on a shoulder of the southern mountains. The rays elongate and shatter against the stippled surface, dressing the river in gold.

In the lower third of the run the river slows, drawing its breath before taking the next bend in a long white rush. The wind dies when the sun sets and the current moves like glass, glinting incandescently where the ripples converge. He can feel the train coming before its headlight burns up the canyon. Its thunder merges with the thunder of the rapids below and builds to a crescendo. He is drowned in this fishing, drowned of everything that was before in his life and oblivious to all that will follow. Somewhere underneath, a great pewter trout completes its journey from the sea, bringing the mystery of the sea, carrying its colors. It will look upward to see his fly. He can feel its presence. One last cast. One last cast. Just one more last cast.

After nightfall, back at the gravel bar where the truck campers park, he takes his coffee pot and walks the rooted path down to the water. Upstream the river is a pulsing rope, frightening at this hour, but in front of him the pool is polished and quiet. Shimmers of reflected light dance on the surface and he watches a minute, baffled. Then he looks up at the night sky, the quarter moon hung and against the horizon a pale shadow that slowly pulses. When he realizes what it is he sets the pot down. Thinking to gain a better vantage, he scrambles up a pinnacle of rock. Waterfalls of milky luminescence pulse more quickly now, flaring against an ebony canvas. Green tendrils of light weave through the celestial current.

And at once he feels his legs cut out from under him. It is a dizzying, swaying sensation, as though he were teetering at the edge of a cliff. A shiver flushes waves of heat through his veins and then suddenly, completely, he is out from under that second skin of age that had insulated him from life and isolated him from himself, and he is simply floating, as exposed to the world as a child.

For a long time he stands there. Then, as the northern lights begin to fade, he feels himself settling back to earth. He climbs down from the rock and picks up his pot of water.

Back at his truck, he sets his lantern burning and cooks his dinner on the tailgate. He whistles a tune above the hiss of the white gas stove, absently staring at the bubbling beans.

"This is the life," he says out loud.

Farther down the bank, four fishermen stand around a campfire. Their voices are lost to the current, but in the flicker of the fire's light he can see one man rocking his arm back and forth, false casting in pantomime. The man sets the hook on an invisible fish, his arm bends over, then suddenly straightens up. He reels in dejectedly. A companion leans back from the waist while his mouth opens in silent laughter. Another holds his hands out to the flame.

He could join them. On a steelhead river a fire is an invitation. But then he doesn't know what it is that they fish for, or if they have to search as deep in the current for it as he does, and anyway, it is too early in the trip to chance the wind their words could stir. Better, he thinks, to hold steady inside the light of the lantern, to feel the ache in his forearm from the rod and keep his mind focused on the hope that awaits the morning.

After all, the river is big. There is room for more than one kind of fisherman. If men come here for other reasons than he does, then the river is kind in that way. It gives what you ask of it.

Except for steelhead.

the headlock manifesto

Lyman Yee

I approached my car to find a red plastic shopping cart resting against the rear bumper.

There are some lazy, inconsiderate jerks in this world and one of them apparently shops at Target. I pushed the cart behind the truck in the next space. I took care to keep it off the truck, which sported a faded "How's My Driving? Dial 1-800-EAT-SHIT" bumper sticker. I unlocked my door. Someone yelled, "Hey, Dick!" Dick is not my name but I turned anyway. He came from the pet store with a clear plastic bag full of water and goldfish in hand. He was a muscular fellow and even the curls of his mullet seemed chiseled and oiled.

"I saw that," he said. "Why don't you put your cart back where you got it, dickweed."

"It's not my cart," I said. "Someone left it here. If you want, just push it into my spot when I leave." He grabbed the cart and sent it rattling across the lot with a kick of his boot, then he knelt and examined his bumper.

"You scratched my bumper, man," he said with sadness.

"I never touched your bumper. Besides, the cart's plastic. Are you kidding?"

"No," he said coolly and stepped closer. I opened my door. He pushed it shut.

Suddenly everything felt like a dream. Half smiling I said, "Look, this whole thing is really silly. I see you've got some goldfish. I love fish too, man."

"I hate fish," he said. "This is food for my turtles."

"I'm sorry, did you just say turtles?" I asked.

My pants had split open through the seat. I felt cool air blowing through my boxers. One side of my face was pressed against the asphalt. I smelled pungent body odor. The turtle man's armpit cupped my ear. We were both on the ground and he applied a classic headlock. I grabbed the cuff of his free arm to keep him from punching me. This angered him, so he tightened the headlock and drove his body weight against my head, against the ground. With one eye open I glanced upon the gentle face of His Holiness the Dalai Lama, his colorful smile and flowing robes framed by the black parking lot pavement. I could also see, next to him, a little goldfish gasping as it flopped rhythmically on the dirty, wet ground. I thought the turtle man was resting when he eased up a bit but it was only to reposition himself. He was trying to choke me. When his sweaty, smelly forearm pushed against the side of my neck I lost it for a moment. I'm done, I thought, and I couldn't help but cry a little bit. The turtle man was talking to me through clenched teeth, spraying saliva into my hair. My ears rang. I couldn't make out his words.

Desperate, I kicked and flailed and looked around for anything that might help me, but all I found were those eyes. Like deep black pools, those eyes of His Holiness the Dalai Lama, and it became his soothing voice I heard inside my head saying so sweetly, ". . . Just breathe . . . just breathe, baby . . . . think good thoughts . . . . "

I closed my eyes and listened to his voice. The throbbing in my ears and head gradually subsided. The smell of body odor and halitosis transformed to the scent of dried desert sage.

The drone of tires on the distant freeway became the rolling silvery slickness that is the Deschutes River. My heavy eyelids absorbed the orange glow of that high lonesome country.

My face felt warm and I rested.

When I opened my eyes I looked out across the river, then downstream at the long slick I was about to fish. I stood and snapped my fly box closed and stuffed it into my vest. I examined the black Egg-Sucking

Leech I had just tied to my leader. It was my own design with a few borrowed ideas; for one thing, I had added a bit of crystal flash in the tail. If I were a steelhead I would kill this thing, I thought.

I started my progression. Fished the water close in before wading into it. Got the rhythm going. Easy cast . . . slight mend . . . dead drift . . . slow swing . . . pause . . . twitch . . . pause . . . a step or two downstream . . . cast . . . .

I don't usually think about much while steelhead fishing. At the end of the day, even on the slowest of days, I never leave with anything brilliant. While at work or while driving in the car I will often have thoughts of places I'd like to visit, or foods I would like to eat, or rivers I would like to fish. But when I'm fishing, I'm just fishing. I fail to recognize hunger and sunburn and only wonder about things like presentation, the speed of the swing and depth. It can sound boring when I analyze it because things really slow down—all thoughts and movements, even my breathing. But at the same time, the days on the river always fly right by.

Halfway through the run I lost my concentration when a beer can floated down the middle of the river. I imagined some rafters upstream, hollering and splashing cold water into each other's faces, which would be reddened with sun and alcohol. Drunken idiots, I thought. I resented their invasion of my paradise. I stopped for a minute and let my fly hang down at the end of the swing. I wet my hand and wiped my face. My head and neck ached then. My tongue was dry and thick. I kept feeling like something wasn't quite right. I heard cars driving by and muted voices in the breeze. I wish they'd shut up, I thought. I turned and looked but didn't see a boat. I did see my fishing partner though, about 50 yards upstream, but he hadn't said anything. I splashed my neck and face again but the water did not refresh. An odor lingered. Something familiar yet grotesque. I felt nauseous. Looking out above the canyon, the skyline suddenly swirled and darkened and suffocated like a fever dream. I could hear the drone of the earth spinning and churning into itself.

"What the hell?" I said. And through the momentary chaos a simple voice said, "Stay with me now . . . just breathe."

Then my rod nearly flew out of my hand. With two hard tugs followed by the beautiful sound of the drag engaging, my fly line vibrated like a tight bowstring. I picked the rod tip up and anticipated a screaming run, but there was nothing. I was hung up. My heart was fluttering. My hands shook and I let out some slack to work the snag. Then I stopped and took a deep breath. I felt good. The chaos, like the take, had vanished as quickly as it appeared.

Well, they're in here, I thought. I worked on the snag. It was stubborn. I pulled from different angles and the line went limp. I reeled up a flyless leader.

"Bummer," I heard someone say. He floated by in a pontoon boat with a pair of casting rods pointing straight up in rod holders, spinners on each reflecting the sun. The man's head was enormous. A foam baseball cap sat much too high atop his head. A salt ring of sweat soaked through it. That hat defies physics, I thought. It cannot possibly stay on. As he floated by I noticed a big red cooler strapped behind his seat and I thought I saw a fish tail pinched under the lid.

I tied on a new fly and cast again. I worked the fly on the swing again and could see through tree branches at the river's edge that the pontoon boat pulled ashore below me. I saw a monofilament arc sail out over the water and even thought I heard it end with a plunk. He was fishing just above the tail-out of my run—my favorite section. I looked upstream to my fishing partner to see if he too had noticed the trespasser. D.L. was in the middle of a glorious roll cast. With effortless motion, two hands on his Spey rod, he must have sent it a hundred feet. The lower lengths of his robes were pulled up and he had tucked them under his waist. The water was just below his white knees. He saw me and smiled and flipped up his polarized clip-ons and his eyes sparkled behind his thick-rimmed glasses. "Just missed one!" he shouted.

I gestured downstream. "You see that?" I asked. He nodded and gave a shrug. He flipped down his lenses and kept fishing. I made two poor casts and stumbled over a large rock. I couldn't resist watching the intruder, cussing him under my breath. "May as well throw a gill net out there with all those treble hooks he's swinging," I muttered. I imagined him chugging a beer, clumsily urinating on an angry rattlesnake. I laughed out loud. Then I witnessed something I never could have imagined.

His rod bent so fiercely that the tip and butt pointed in the same direction. His reel paid out line for what seemed like a minute straight and then a turbulence erupted in the middle of the river as if Godzilla himself were about to surface. I couldn't stand it. I stepped out onto the bank, unwilling to give the man the satisfaction of seeing me watching him. D.L. stopped fishing too and came over to sit next to me on a log.

"That's a big mother," he said.

"I expect it is," I said. We gawked as the giant steelhead went completely airborne three times in succession.

"That just makes me sick," I said. "It was obvious we were fishing downstream."

"Maybe he didn't know," D.L. said.

"He knew. But even if he didn't, there's only about a million miles of water here, and he has to fish right next to us?"

"We are social animals, really."

I looked at him.

"Sorry," he said, and smiled.

"Does anything ever bother you?" I asked.

"Sure it does. I am just a man, remember. I get angry or sad like any other man. My people live in oppression, remember? And I've been in exile for a long, long time. This," he said, looking out across the canyon, "this is all just sun and sky and hooks and water. We're just fishing, man. Just like he is. Just go with it."

"I know," I said.

"You read my book yet?"

"The back cover. Table of contents," I said. "I just got it, remember?"

"It's all in there, man."

The steelhead was tiring and the man fought it well, steering it away from the rocky water below the tail-out. The fish trudged steadily upstream and the man walked up with it. He stood in the water right before us.

"This thing's strong," he said.

"You got him," I said. "Nice and easy."

D.L. held a disposable camera. He nudged me with it. "How's this thing work?" he asked. He handed it to me and I got up and took some action shots of the man landing his steelhead. The fish came in close and the man finally tailed it and he knelt down and cradled the thing gently and deliberately, like a father holding his newborn for the first time.

"This is the biggest fish I've ever seen," he said. It was magnificent. A large buck nearing 20 pounds. And when the waves and sun caught the steelhead's chromed sides just right, a magnificent streak of pink faded in and out, like he was blushing at his own beauty.

"Big smile," I said and he obliged. I took the hook out for him. It just about fell out on its own—a single barbless hook at the end of a spoon. He held the fish in the shallows, reviving it, praising it, then let it go.

"Not a keeper?" I baited.

"I never keep them," he said.

"Me neither."

"I'm a vegetarian anyway."

"Me too," said D.L. They smiled at each other and nodded in approval. "Well I better get me one of those," D.L. continued. "Nice job." He headed upstream and re-cinched his garments about his waist along the way.

"Something to remember it by," I said and handed the man the camera. "Got some good ones I think."

"Oh, wow. Thanks. I don't know what to say."

"Don't worry about it."

"Hey I'm sorry I walked him right up through your spot. I just didn't want him to take off on me downstream."

"I would have done the same thing. You fought him really well. You're a good fisherman."

"Oh, that's nothing compared to what you're doing. That looks impossible."

We stopped and watched D.L. a while. The loops and rolls of his fly line were like something living, something synchronous, breathing with the soft shadows of his draped robes.

"It's really not as hard as it looks," I said.

"It looks beautiful," he said, "but I'm kind of lazy. It just seems like a lot of work."

I thought about what I should say then. I wanted to say something sage-like, something heroic. I wanted to sound like D.L.

With every cast the possibility of perfection arises. That brief moment when randomness ceases to exist and time and the universe stop to enjoy the beauty of your struggle. That pristine balance of love and loss, of hope and terror radiating from a single point at the end of a clear strand of line, up through your trembling hands and body and into your very heart, leaving it overflowing with God's best intentions.

That's what I wanted to say but it didn't come to me just then. So I just told him that it's all worth it. The hours or days or even years of casting are worth a moment of life perfected.

"I suppose it is," he said.

"Well, I guess I'll hit the water again," I said.

"Well, hey. Thanks for the pictures," he said. "You're not like most fly fishermen I've seen. They're usually a little uptight, you know. No offense."

"It's all pretty much the same. We're all just fishermen."

He gave me his hand to shake and when I took it he just stared at me for some time. Then he pulled me in slowly and hugged me. I patted his shoulder blade, awkwardly, then hugged him back. He squeezed me tighter and I felt his heartbeat. I smelled his sweat.

"I can't breathe," I said and he let go and drew back and looked at me.

"Are you okay?" he asked. I didn't answer. His round face and the sky around it faded white.

I opened my eyes. I was lying down. The asphalt cooled my back. I could hear nothing beyond my ears ringing. A woman in a white-collared shirt leaned over me. A paramedic. She spoke slowly with exaggerated gestures. I read her lips.

"Can you hear me? Are you okay?"

I looked around and saw things in a peculiar light, like props on a stage. I noticed a rusty exhaust pipe. A large truck bumper. A toddler in a red shopping cart. An elderly woman talking to a police officer. The officer nodding and scribbling notes. A small crowd of worried faces staring back at me.

My hearing returned slowly. I could hear my breathing. Then the cars from the road, the policeman's radio.

"Can you hear me?" the woman said. "You were unconscious. Can you hear me? Sir, do you understand what happened to you?"

Yes, I thought, but could not speak. I felt a calmness right then and I didn't want anything to spoil it. I just needed to lie still, completely relaxed, as I enjoyed for a moment longer such good, good thoughts.

the surrender

Bil Monan

Y ou could tell by the arrival of staff officers on the line. They usually appeared in pairs, stepped out of their jeeps, looked officious and, if they were lucky, would be shelled by less then accurate German mortars. They would then quickly remount and run like hell to the rear, all the while congratulating themselves on getting the Combat Infantry Badge and perhaps the Bronze Star.

My platoon, all of 20 men, more like a glorified squad, had been dug in along the edge of a stream in western Austria for four days. It was a luxury of sorts, since it was unusual for us to be so static. Everything was moving fast and resistance, though sporadic, was still lethal, and none of us had any urge to be the last casualty. The one good thing was that it appeared the Germans felt the same way overall. We had been sent forward to this stream, the Erlauf, near the town of Scheibbs, to ensure that the bridge was secure and to hold the position until we were relieved. At first, the Germans fired a few mortar rounds and a volley of machine gun fire to let us know they were indeed on the other side, but had since been silent.

I looked down the line where my men had dug in and could only see piles of dirt with eyes—mud soldiers. At this point you could probably throw seed on them and grow crops. No longer did they have names. It was just "You, You and You, over there," "You and You, that way," and "You, stay here." To my men I was just "Lieutenant." Only Sergeant Malvani had a name, and it was "Conductor."

He was an unlikely sergeant—scrawny, short, glasses and very long, elegant fingers. He had been a concert violinist back home and had been 4F'd early on, but after Normandy and all the losses, the draft board eventually decided he was just perfect. We called him the Conductor after he lost two fingers to shrapnel somewhere in the Ardennes and, upon discovering his loss, he remarked that his violin days were over and he would become a conductor. He never spoke of it again. It was what made him such a good sergeant; he just adapted and made stuff happen.

We weren't at all similar, Malvani and I. He was actually a city boy and relatively sophisticated, and I was just an ROTC graduate from Westkill, New York. The only symphony I had ever heard was the thunder in the Catskills and the tumbling of water over rocks on the Willowemoc. But we were similar on one account: We had both been promoted primarily for surviving. The only thing that bothered me about Sgt. Malvani was that he wore a helmet into which a bullet had entered on the left side before somehow miraculously spinning across the front casing and exiting through the right.

I said to him, "Sergeant, you need to dump that helmet. It only reinforces the men's belief that their leaders have no brains."

"Well, me accepting these sergeant stripes just proves they're right." I left it alone, but it gave me the creeps.

After a while, it struck me that it really had gotten quiet. I mean, I was actually thinking. I could not remember a time over the last year when my brain wasn't being banged from one side of my skull to the other by artillery fire. I decided to peek over the edge of my foxhole to scan the other side of the stream. I saw nothing moving, which was normal. You never saw anyone out front—not anyone alive, that is. What I did notice was the stream.

To my left it made a broad turn back toward the German lines, where it channeled deep and close to a steep rock wall. As it flowed toward me it straightened out and formed a nice, flat pool about 50 yards long and 50 yards wide, just at the place where both of our lines faced one another. The stream ran down to my right under the bridge and faded into the darkness created by a canopy of overhanging trees. The milky, green-tinged water ran fast and cold. The Esopus, back home in the Catskills, had the same look in early spring and I began to see in each pocket of water and riffle a place where, with the right presentation and the right fly, a nice brown trout would come roaring out of the water. I started to see Junction Pool at Roscoe, where the Little Beaverkill merges with the Willowemoc and where the late evening hatch would emerge and all hell would break loose as trout gorged on Green Drakes or Blue Quills or something else that I usually could never match.

Now, while you might expect most men in my situation to be thinking of women, most of us had lost our libidos somewhere between the first hundred yards of beach in Normandy and the hedgerows on the Rhine. But thoughts of trout I could handle. I remembered my dad teaching me how to fly-fish on the little Westkill, which ran right behind our house. The first trout I caught on a fly was a beautiful 12-inch native brook. I used a brown dry fly. My dad didn't have any names for the flies. He just said, "Match the damn color as best you can or make something up that's black with a little red on it." And that's what we did. Working in our garage at night, pulling feathers from grouse capes, cutting up deerskins, and even slicing little chunks of wool from our socks, we would make our flies. My mom thought we had a terrible moth problem.

I thought about Fir Brook and how my dad and I would head up high when it had rained enough for the Willowemoc and Beaverkill to run fast and muddy. The Fir was a small stream, hard to fish, and it dropped into a small gorge that required you to commit most of a day working small pockets of water behind boulders and little waterfalls. We would use about five feet of line and just flick it over a rock into any likely spot, and the brook trout would strike like piranhas on a wounded pig. We only used tiny black ants, since the average trout was about eight inches, but I do believe a pig cast just right would have provoked those greedy little brookies to strike as well.

My reverie was aborted by a sharp slap to the back of my helmet and a voice so close to my ear that the strident whisper sounded like shell fire, saying, "Wake up, Lieutenant, something's moving across the stream!"

I stared hard across the stream and noticed pieces of loose shale and dirt slipping down the face of the embankment from a thick hedge. A German soldier slid down the bank and took a few tentative steps towards the edge of the stream.

Sergeant Malvani raised his M-1. I grabbed the end of his rifle and said, "Hold off, Sergeant; when have you ever seen a living German out front? They haven't shot at us for three days. Tell the men to hold their fire."

Sergeant Malvani looked at me like I was insane, but waved down the men. We waited and watched.

The soldier righted himself with some difficulty; apparently he had a bad left leg. He proceeded to remove his helmet and camouflage poncho, then quite deliberately folded the poncho, neatly laid it on the gravel streambed and placed his helmet on top.

He wore no insignia, but it was obvious that he was an officer. How I knew, I couldn't tell you. He just held himself in a certain way. Most line officers, myself included, had learned long ago not to wear anything that might distinguish us—snipers made short work of you if you did. He was unarmed and wore the uniform of the Wehrmacht, not the SS, which was a relief in some ways. Not that the Wehrmacht didn't try to kill you; they just seemed more like us, less fanatic. He was a handsome man, stood about six foot, lean, but then there were not many fat soldiers these days. He was an older man, late 40's perhaps, at least that was my perspective, since he had graying hair around his temples kind of like my dad. He then turned back to the bank, reached up into the hedges and proceeded to pull something out of the bushes.

Once again Sergeant Malvani raised his rifle and once again I pushed it down.

I said, "It's not a rifle he's getting, Sergeant."

"What in the hell is he getting?" replied Malvani.

"It's a fly rod."

"He must be shell shocked," Malvani exclaimed.

"No, I think he's just tired of this war."

Again, we just waited and watched. There was a certain choreography to the officer's actions. I suspected he knew that his life depended on carefully orchestrated movements, so everything he did seemed to flow with a cautious slow motion. Reaching into his field jacket he produced a green felt Tyrolean hat. There was a pheasant feather stuck in the hatband and around the sides there were a number of trout flies hooked haphazardly into the felt. He pulled off a fly that looked like some kind of streamer. All I could see was a flash of whitish silver with a blackish body. He tied the fly to his leader, then stuck the hat on his head, reached into his tunic again and removed a pipe. With deliberate nonchalance he tapped the bowl on some rocks to remove the old ashes, filled the pipe, lit it, and with obvious enjoyment took a few puffs. Picking up the rod, he stepped to the edge of the stream while stripping off line, and started to false cast to extend the line out over the stream. All this orchestration came to an abrupt end on one of his back casts, when the fly ended up snagged on a low branch jutting out from the hedge line behind him. Apparently, he was out of practice.

I heard a laugh next to me. Malvani thought it was funny. I mean, so did I, but being a fisherman I couldn't help but feel sorry for the man. It's okay to snag when you are by yourself, but to have an audience can be demoralizing. It's kind of like being in a spelling contest in third grade and in front of all your peers and parents and you misspell a simple word like "castle," which I once did.

Retrieving the fly, the fishing soldier, dressed in combat gray, black boots and green hat, went unperturbedly about the business of catching fish. The birds started moving, and perhaps Malvani's laugh allowed everything to exhale, for the air seemed relaxed and alive again.

He worked to my left, casting up and across where the stream made the turn towards the flat water in our front. His streamer fell lightly on the edge of the far bank. The lure caught the current where the last bit of rapids tailed into a softening pool, and just as the streamer reached the apex of its turn in the current, a roiling of water marked the strike of a hungry brown trout. With little fanfare, but with elegant precision, the soldier worked the fish to his boot. The fish was about 12 inches long and plump. He picked it up, broke its neck and plopped it on the gravel bar near the bank.

The man knew how to fish. He worked the water with such effortless skill that he caught fish after fish in every likely spot. The fly went exactly where he wanted it to go. Using a series of long casts, roll casts, even short whip-like backhand casts when he wanted to flip it under a low branch or cut bank, he worked the stream like a farmer gleaning his fields. The trout seemed endless in their quantity and maybe a little stupid. More than likely they hadn't been fished for years and had no experience with a hook, but maybe I was just jealous and didn't want to admit that the man was flat-out good. I noticed that he only kept trout of about 10 to 12 inches in length. When he landed a few that were larger he gently released them.

I found myself mesmerized, and by now he had worked down the stream so that he was only 20 yards off to my left. I could clearly see the streamer flashing in the water. I noticed directly below me a fallen tree that had formed a good-size hole. Swirling in the eddy where the current broke around the end of the trunk there lay the dark shadow of a trout about 20 inches long. Staggered around it hovered a number of smaller trout like P-51 Mustangs protecting a B-17 bomber; I guess a flight of Messerschmidts protecting a Junkers bomber would be more like it, the trout being Austrian. Every time the streamer passed outside the edge of the pool, the large fish would move up to a staging point to consider a strike, but then his smaller cousins would race out and attack the fly. This fish was wise. He would let the small ones in their greed go charging off to their demise and he would just slip back and wait. He wasn't in a hurry and he didn't want to work that hard.

I couldn't stand it. The soldier's fly was drifting about one foot short. I stood up. God does make fools and here I was—a magnificent example. I think Malvani passed out. I was standing, totally exposed. I don't think I had stood erect for a year. I had come to feel like an ape, always running at a crouch. Not only did I stand up in the face of the enemy, I was also gesticulating with my arms. I pointed straight down at the trout and then put my hands about 20 inches apart.

I wasn't shot. The soldier looked up, nodded his head and dropped down a few feet and out into the stream. The streamer drifted perfectly into the edge of the eddy and the old trout went for it. It struck hard. The soldier set the hook, and upon feeling the sting the fish broke water and flung itself violently back and forth. It is unusual for a brown to leap much, but this one did. The battle was waged fairly, the angler giving line as the trout tried to roar down stream. Then keeping pressure, allowing no slack, stripping line, with the rod tip high, the soldier tired the old fish down. He didn't horse it around but brought the fish to heel as quickly as possible. He bent down and with both hands brought the fish up to chest height and held it out to show me. It was a beautiful brown with bright red splotches sprinkled amidst coal black spots all splashed against a greenish, blue-gray background. It was an old fish with a hooked jaw and square head, the brood master of the stream.

The fisherman then ever so gently swished the big fish in the current to revive it and let it go. He stood, looked my way and waved me towards him. Without hesitation, I shouldered my rifle and began to slip down the bank toward the stream. Sergeant Malvani gave me a hard look and said, "You're not really going?"

I replied with a curt "Yes."

"You're an idiot," retorted Malvani.

I gave him a hard look back.

"Sir."

I met him halfway across the stream where the water came to about our shins. It was so brutally cold that it made your teeth ache. I looked at the bank where he had laid out about 15 trout and said, " Trout," and he replied, "Forellen."

He saluted and said, "I am Leutnant Franz Meyers."

"Lieutenant Patrick Skimmin," I said, and I returned the salute.

"Leutnant Skimmin, for me this war is over and my men are hungry. Perhaps your soldiers are hungry, too?" And he handed me the rod.

Good, I thought, he speaks English. They all spoke English it seemed, and I can only say, "*Hande hoch*" and "*nicht schissen*" in German.

I took the rod, looked at him and said, "Aren't you kind of old to be a lieutenant?"

"All the young men are buried in Russia. I was invalided for wounds during the First World War, but was called up to form a Volkssturm unit to protect my village and this bridge. All my soldiers are 15-year-old boys or old men like me. I have no great ambition to die or have my village destroyed for Germany since I am Austrian."

I turned to the stream, stripped line and proceeded to cast, slowly remembering all the mechanics of the sport I so loved. It was the one way I could always find peace and quiet, and I had forgotten what that was like. I caught as he did, but made a point to catch 25 trout since I had counted 15 of his. I think we both knew we were lying about how many men we were feeding.

As I laid the last trout on the shore, Franz Meyers came to me and with strict military formality said, "I surrender my weapons, my men and my village to the United States Army, and to you Patrick Skimmin, I surrender the stream.

Franz turned to his side of the stream and waved to the hedges. Within seconds 10 gray-clad scarecrows tumbled to the streambed, armed with 12-inch frying pans, mess kits, potatoes, cabbages and onions. I waved to my men and the same mass scrambling and confusion ensued as my 20 mud-soldiers emerged with American cigarettes and chocolate. On that night, on the edge of the Erlauf, we shared a most glorious fish fry. And it was here, as it was for Franz Meyers, that my war ended.

tex, mex, and the amazons

Rhett Ashley

He had flown over Alaskan rivers with Dr. Seuss names: The Sit-Up; the Cat's-Lick; the Sly-You; and we were circling the beach at the mouth of the Chick-Cluck. At least that's what I thought I heard.

I was not a happy camper. We had missed our flight to King Salmon, which meant the rafting expedition had departed without us, and now an accommodating bush pilot was negotiating our addition to a camp of women fly fishers. I could only imagine a twittering bunch of bubbleheads.

The pilot was gleefully describing us on the radio as "Two little chicks that need a mother hen. They aren't exactly Seven Sisters co-eds, but neither are they lady mud-rasslers." (This was to make the ladies down below believe we were girls.) "Take them in and you get two cases of Oregon Glint Ridge Pinot Gris." (No immediate answer.) "And, um, a box of king crab."

I did not like any of this. And yet the alternative of returning to Anchorage was too depressing even to think about.

("We" meant myself and a banged-up bull rider from Texas I had been stuck with on all flights since El Paso. "Texicans" we call them in New Mexico. You know the type: Too-big hat. Too-big belt buckle. Pterodactyl-hide cowboy boots.)

But as the pilot tipped his wings for the landing and I saw salmon stacked up like cordwood, my attitude changed. Even if I'd missed the rafting expedition there were fish in the rivers and I was going to catch the hell out of them. The plane bounced along the beach and taxied to a stop about 300 yards from a small tent camp. The pilot hurriedly unloaded and was back in the air before the first female arrived on an ATV with a 12-gauge semiautomatic shotgun slung across her back. She was not a twittering bubblehead. Though auburn-haired and not unattractive, she was as sinewy as a leather strap, and she spoke with military abruptness.

"You aren't women."

"Course we ain't," drawled Texas.

"We were told AirOrca was dropping two women."

"Well, we ain't them."

"Then you can't stay here. Can't fish here. Can't do anything here."

"Hey, we can't leave," I pointed out. "There's glaciers to the north; the Pacific to our backs. There's no roads. No ferries. We're stuck here until the plane comes to pick up the lot of us. We're just here to fish."

She zoomed back to the tents to parley with the other gals, and after a few minutes the four of them trooped down the beach toward us. The blonde one was huge—about six-one, with hands big enough to palm a basketball. Of the remaining two, one was petite, with high cheekbones and a string of bear claws around her neck, while the other was built like a body builder and had a big, shiny raven's feather protruding from her prematurely graying hair. They stood shoulder to shoulder and glared at us as if thinking about using us in a human sacrifice.

"Now listen up. We are the High and Dry Flyfishers. Every one of us has been divorced at least once, and all of us came up here hoping— and I mean really, really hoping—not to see a man for an entire week. In fact, when we heard that the only available guides were a couple of pretty-boys from Montana, we decided to go it alone out here instead. So maybe now you have an idea of the trouble you're in."

The silent, murderous glaring resumed for a long moment before she finally said, "I'm Cappy; me and the big girl here, Dallas, are ex-Navy officers. We share a veterinary practice. Sissy's a psychiatrist. Stitch is a surgeon." As I was trying to memorize their names—Big Dallas was easy; Sissy, the shrink, was the one with the cheekbones, and Stitch was the muscle-bound one—Cappy said, "Now what and who are you?"

Tex gave them all a big, oblivious grin. "Wal, I'm mostly a bull rider. But sometimes steers. Sometimes broncs. Right now I'm resting various broke and strained body parts. Call me Tex."

"And you?"

"I'm a rancher," I said. "Apples, not cows. From New Mexico."

"Tex and Mex," someone laughed.

Here Dallas interrupted and poked an astonishingly long finger at us. "Figure out your own sleeping arrangements. Here are the rules: First, stay out of our way. Second, all dry flies. Third, what you come with is what you fish with. We don't loan you any gear; don't even ask.

"You'll have your own beat each day, but we will check for infractions. Lastly, stay out of our way. Any questions?"

"None here," I said.

Tex, who had been staring at Dallas with unconcealed fascination, smiled and said, "I got one. Is everything real up there on the balcony?"

I was stunned. Even for a Texican that was crass.

The large veterinarian blushed; she took a step away, then backstepped and snapped a vicious elbow into his ribs. "How's your mezzanine?" she retorted after Tex had yelled in surprise and doubled over.

Cappy barked, "Dammit, Dallas, you learned nothing in those anger management classes!"

"Dammit yourself, Captain. You heard what he said." She glared at me, "What are you grinning at?"

"I just love seeing Texicans put in their place."

"I'm from Texas myself, and I'd be happy to clean your clock, too. Can you wash dishes?"

"Well, I haven't. . . ."

"Good. Then follow me. It's my night to cook."

After supper, there was a Pinot Gris period of jollity, but Tex and I were not offered any wine. Tex wandered off in a sulk, his arm pressed against his injured ribs. I sat by myself and listened to roaring rounds of toasts, one of which was made in tribute to "The Elbow." I eventually sidled up to Sissy, who I found to be the least intimidating of the four. Sissy had produced a vise and a laptop tying bench and was wrapping

Pollywogs. After a while she let me try my hand, but I couldn't seem to get the hang of spinning pink deer hair. Mostly, I just pretended to tie while eavesdropping on the surrounding conversation. An inebriated lady mentioned boating: three of them had rowed in college. Martial arts? All of them had studied Tai Chi, Shorin Ryu, or kick-boxing. Exotic fishing? Patagonia, New Zealand, Kamchatka, Iceland.

Amazing ladies. I felt inadequate—small, you might even say—in comparison.

"Tie basically anything, as long as it's a dry fly," Sissy explained, apparently failing to notice that my first bundle of deer hair had exploded in my fingers and now lay scattered all around me on the gravel. "It has to be a dry. After all, it's the High and Dry Flyfishers."

I hadn't brought a single dry fly. "Can I have just one 'Wog?" I wheedled.

"No."

I quickly changed the subject.

"When you are toasting, I hear 'Twobeedee' and 'Threebeedee.' What's a 'Threebeedee'?"

She laughed. "B.D. is shorthand for baker's dozen. Like, a 'Three-beedee' would be about 40 salmon."

Then Cappy stalked over and broke up the fun. "Rules, Sissy. Remember? No coaching. No coddling. No flies. No materials."

I walked away feeling lonely and lost. I climbed up onto an old water tank platform to see what kind of bed site it would make. Perhaps I could roll my sleeping bag up inside a tarp like a burrito, and at least be safe from the rain and dew. I wondered if I would count bears in my sleep.

The next day I sneaked out and tried fishing with forbidden wet flies. They did not work. I tried swimming them; weighting them; tying them in tandem. Finally I gave up and just beachcombed, eventually finding a whalebone on the beach.

The second day was as fishless as the first. I tried exciting the fish by tossing rocks at them—after all, it works for Jim Teeny, doesn't it? I tried chumming them with bits of sandwich. I tried dapping for them with nymphs. Not a single take.

On the third morning I decided dryfly thievery was the solution. I waited until everyone had left camp, then poked my head into their tents. Not a single fly. Damn. I would have to tie my own dry flies—but with what?

Tex walked up. "Hey, pardner. Look what I got." He held up feathers. "I got hooks and thread. If you got fur or foam, we're in bidness."

I remembered I had foam ear plugs. "I've got foam. Did you notice the wolf-fur hood on Cappy's parka?"

"Yeah." He was grinning. "And she wasn't wearing it this morning when she left."

Later we were hunkered down with a fly clamped in the pliers of Tex's Swiss Army knife. We threaded the hook through the earplug, cemented it in place with Liquid Bandage, spun a feather around the body, and tied in a wolf-hair tail.

I looked at it dubiously. "It looks like an earplug with some feathers and fur."

"Maybe to us it does. But it don't look like an earplug to a salmon 'cause he ain't never seen one. Let's tie up the whole package of twelve."

Tex held the pliers and I tied while he gave me an update on his personal war with the Amazons, as he called them. "You know those locked-in salmon in the Sigh-You braid? Well, I been catching 'em for two days. This morning Dallas caught me there using wets. Hell, they were only gonna die there, so why not catch 'em, don't you agree?"

I didn't. My gut feeling was you shouldn't harass a stressed fish. I shook my head and said nothing.

"Dallas gave me hell. Called me a bunch of names that hurt my feelings. Then she broke my rod."

"You're kidding, right?" I was shocked.

He looked rueful. "No. I said something smartass and she broke it."

"You didn't go ballistic?"

"Actually, I was awed. Angry women are like rodeo bulls or mustangs. All spirit, y'know?"

"That's ridiculous."

"No, it ain't. You have to break 'em. High-strung women, I mean. Like you do mustangs. Mustangs ain't worth a damn 'til you break 'em."

"Women aren't horses. And if she was a horse you couldn't afford to stable her, anyway. Question is: how are you going to fish without a rod?"

He gave me his best cowboy smile. Pure Gene Autry. "Why, share yours, of course! I can cast farther than you. So you let me cast. Then I hand the rod to you. You play him in. I rassel him to shore. Teamwork. Just like team roping."

I opened my mouth to argue, then realized I had not caught a single fish. "I want to catch one. Just one. For the family album."

Tex laughed. "All it takes is technique."

"How come you got technique and I don't?"

"Cause I spied on the Amazons and figgered out their technique," he said. "That cliff, what they call The Bluffs? We'll peek over. If an Amazon is down there, you watch and I'll explain it."

Indeed, Stitch, the muscular kick-boxing surgeon, was below us. We could see about 70 salmon amassed in front of her. A few fish nosed about the sides of the river.

Tex whispered, "The middle fish are not the takers. The fish near the banks are the takers. Stitch will cast over the middle fish to the ones next to the bank. Now, the important thing to remember is: The fly is like a piece of yarn you tease a cat with. A cat won't snatch it until it's twitched. Look, Stitch is putting the fly up to the bank, letting the fly drift down a few feet. See that fish about three feet downstream? Stitch will start her twitch pretty soon."

When Stitch twitched, the salmon stiffened and, like an arrow, pointed itself at the fly. "Pure instinct," Tex whispered. "Pure predator impulse."

On the second twitch the fish was in motion and on the third twitch it opened its mouth and engulfed the fly. "There," whispered Tex. "She waits until the mouth comes down on the fly. See? There's only about a half second to set the hook. Watch; she sets the hook, then jerks back about three times for insurance."

It was, to me, a dawning. A revelation. An epiphany.

We crept back several feet to where Stitch couldn't see us.

I was incredulous. All the missing parts to the puzzle. Except Pink Pollywogs. "You think our. . . ?"

"You BigTimeBetcha! No more wets. We got our own dries now. Ear Wogs!"

"Ear Wigs!" I offered as a better name. We both laughed then, remembering Stitch below us, stifled our glee.

We hiked down near the mouth, well away from any Amazons. We waded out with my rod. Tex let a lot of line out, then jerked it into the air, did a lot of lasso-type circles while I ducked, then fired it over to the other bank. He handed the rod to me and began a litany of instructions: "Let it drift six feet or so. Now, twitch. Another four seconds. Now twitch."

Bam! I was so startled I didn't set the hook. Tex gave a sarcastic look at his watch.

"Okay, strike any time now."

"Sorry." I handed him the rod. "Let's do it again."

This time I hunched forward, watching intently for the take. Sure enough, on the third twitch the nose came up and swallowed the fly. This time I was ready and set the hook. Then began a comedy of errors— bumping, shoving, dodging, getting line-tangled—but somehow we got the fish in. Then we began to argue about the sex. If the mouth is farther back than the eye. If the nose is hooked. If the belly is rounder. On some fish it was just hard to tell.

"It would be so easy if fish had balls," Tex lamented.

We took pictures, each of us posing with the salmon, then released it. Beginner's luck, I thought, but then we landed another, and another. Seven fish chewed up the first fly, so we put on a second one. After a dozen salmon we didn't bother to count anymore.

"It doesn't matter," Tex said, "we would just lie about it anyway."

That evening there was a big bonfire and the High and Dry crew toasted each other. "Twobeedee," was called, and "Threebeedee" was shouted back.

I was considering announcing our breakthrough when Tex strolled up with a long piece of frayed rope he'd tied into a loop. He was tossing it around and snagging any little thing that resembled a horn. He winked at me and I had a sudden premonition of trouble.

Dallas had just announced a Fourbeedee and stepped forward to clink glasses when Tex's loop dropped over her shoulders. He jerked the rope, pulled a pigging string from his back pocket as she fell, and proceeded to whip a tie around her ankles and then her wrists. Then he leaped up and shouted, "Six seconds flat."

He bent back down and was whispering something in her ear when all hell broke loose. The three women still standing went berserk. Someone pulled me down from behind. Someone else tied my feet, and I couldn't get back up. As soon as I was immobilized the screaming women piled on Tex. In less than a minute both of us were lying with our faces in the gravel and our hands tied behind our backs.

The women untrussed Dallas, then the four of them grabbed bottles of wine and whiskey and went running up the beach, leaping and howling and drinking straight from the bottle in celebration of their triumph.

The two of us struggled a while before resigning ourselves to our situation. Tex started musing. "You know, I don't heal quite like I used to. I've got to give up rodeo before it kills me."

I opined, "You probably won't quit until they carry you out on a stretcher."

After a long silence he asked, "What is it about orcharding that you like?"

"The quiet. Just me and the trees."

"Sounds boring. Nice though. How long you done it?"

"About ten years. It's been in the family about fifty. On a bad year I'd sell it in a flash if somebody offered me half what it's worth."

We lay there in silence listening to the sounds of revelry growing farther and farther away. Much later, Sissy came back alone to untie us. "I did a little rodeoing in college," she chirped. "I tied you up quicker'n you did Dallas."

"Now how come that don't surprise me?" Tex said.

Next morning there was a new, relaxed atmosphere in camp. People smiled. Cappy assigned us the best beat. And by noon Tex and I had caught and released almost 30 salmon. We started walking back to camp in high spirits. We had scored a Twobeedee.

As we neared the place called The Bluff we heard a tremendous splashing below. We crawled to the edge and looked down. A rope hung over the spot where Dallas had climbed down. She was playing a big salmon.

"My gawd, it's huge," croaked Tex. "Just look at the size of him. He's half again bigger'n the others."

We didn't notice the quaking willows at first; nor did Dallas down below. But as the brown bear emerged and headed directly toward her at a trot, we began yelling. Following a moment of paralysis, I knelt down and kicked my legs over the edge of the drop-off, fortunately finding a foothold on the first try, and then began picking my way down the steep rock face with the idea in mind of distracting the bear once I reached the beach. For his part, Tex heroically grabbed the rope and swung Tarzan-like down the cliff. But on perhaps the third big swing, the rope twisted and he spun into a boulder with a stiff leg. You could see the knee buckle and he let go of the rope and fell face forward, reaching out with his arms to break the fall. As he hit, the elbow of his right arm snapped and collapsed. And yet he still got up and staggered forward.

When Dallas finally realized what was happening, she hesitated for only a split second, then turned and charged toward Tex. She caught him with a shoulder in the mid-section and he doubled over like a sack of grain. This slowed her, but she continued to run ploddingly toward the rope. As I leaped the final five feet to the beach I heard her giving commands to Tex: "Grab my belt in back. Keep your weight centered on my shoulders and, for Pete's sake, don't try to help. Let me do it all." Then she was carrying him up the rope with slow, straining, hand-over-hand pulls, her studded wading boots giving added grip and lift.

Meanwhile, I was discovering that my plan to distract the bear had worked only too well. Though the animal had slowed to a fast walk, it was coming straight at me with a look in its eyes that was anything but playful, and I had no place to go. I glanced about for a log or a stick—anything to put between me and the bear. But there were only rocks. I grabbed two grapefruit-size rocks and began banging them together. And screaming. That's what I had read somewhere: Face a brown bear head on, make noise and don't run. So I screamed and banged the rocks together like a crazed caveman. For naught; the bear kept coming.

I was dizzy. I felt faint. My vision clouded with tears.

About six feet away, the bear skidded to a halt. Up close, the smell alone was enough to make me retch, but the long talons and dirty teeth scared me more. When he flattened his ears and growled, I panicked.

I threw the rock in my right hand at his head. It struck him in the ruff and he hardly noticed it. The second rock thrown with my left hand completely missed him. And then the sweetest sound in the whole world reached my ears:

The boom of Cappy's 12-gauge.

On the first boom the bear swung his head, slinging snot and slobber on my face, and on the second boom he turned and ran. I collapsed to a kneeling position in the sand and shook for several minutes. I eventually climbed very slowly up the rope, hyperventilating all the while.

On top Sissy greeted me cheerfully. "I got it all on digital camera. Can you believe it all happened in less than two minutes?"

Dallas was strapping Tex onto the ATV luggage rack. She patted him occasionally. He looked meek. She looked calm. Their relationship had clearly changed.

Cappy sat in the ATV saddle, reloading the shotgun. "He's hurt bad," she said matter-of-factly.

Back at camp Tex was tended to. They swarmed over him, binding his leg, splinting his elbow, bringing him hot tea. Most of the actual medical work was undertaken by Cappy and Dallas rather than by Stitch, the people-doctor. Fitting, I thought, veterinarians working on "rough stock."

All the women tisked and clucked and cooed when Tex admitted that the same knee had been busted twice before. They gasped with admiration when he refused to allow them to radio for an evacuation plane.

He said, "Hell, I been hurt worse 'n this, and climbed back in the saddle the very same day." This was an obvious lie, but they gasped nonetheless, and suddenly I felt a stab of intense jealousy. Why weren't they oo-ing and cooing about me? I was the one who'd stood up to the bear—even if it had been just a small, three-year-old juvenile.

An irate "Well, I guess David who stands up to Goliath deserves no credit, eh, girls?" slipped out of me. This outburst probably surprised me more than it surprised them, but they stopped their ministrations and looked at me curiously. Finally Stitch chuckled and began singing:

"Who's our hero? Alley Oop. Alley Oop. Who's our hero? Alley Oop."

Embarrassed, I fled down the beach.

On the last night, after supper, the women crowded around the digital camera. Sissy cooed, "Look at Oop; how brave!" But mostly they ran and re-ran the crumpling of Tex's leg. It seemed to fascinate them.

Finally came the magic question: "How'd you do fishing today?"

In unison Tex and I shouted, "Twobeedee!" They all looked at us.

"On what?" Cappy was suspicious.

"On our very own dries," bragged Tex, who had spent the entire day coaching me from the seat of Cappy's ATV. He pulled a fly off his Stetson to show them.

"It's an earplug!" the women chorused gleefully.

"Ear Wog," Tex corrected.

"Ear Wig," I argued.

"Twobeedee on this little thing?"

"Absolutely," I replied.

Then the toasts started. Wine, brandy, whiskey.

Later, an inebriated Cappy asked, "Are you two cowguys, cowgoons, cowbouys both divorced?"

"Yes," I answered.

"Twice over," Tex said.

She laughed and said, "Then you're both High and Dry foosher . . . fishergoons, too!"

Later, Cappy, Sissy and Stitch were assailing me with new, drunken verses of the "Alley Oop" song when Dallas and Tex appeared, she supporting him with an arm around his waist.

"Oop," said Dallas almost bashfully, "We want to buy your orchard."

I didn't know what to say at first. "It loses money three years out of 10, you know."

Dallas merely shrugged. "That's all right. All that means to me is snipping a few more love-sacks off of golden retrievers named 'Lucky.'"

I felt a sarcastic reply was in order. Something like, "A lot of money won't turn you Texicans into New Mexicans."

But I didn't say it, because I suddenly recognized that Tex and Dallas had morphed into a civil, almost sweet, couple—thereby proving, perhaps, that two jerks can cancel each other out, at least temporarily.

In a serious voice I said, "In New Mexico there's a saying: 'Sell your land, sell your mamma.' I can't sell you my orchard.

"However,"—I looked at their clasped hands—"I know of a few other orchards that might bow to the pressure of a lot of cash."

Suddenly Tex and Dallas were hugging me and calling me "Oop" and, more disturbingly, "neighbor." They were laughing and putting their hands on each other's butts when they thought no one was looking. And they were dreaming aloud about orchards and apples and the possibility of relationships that did not end in anger and bitter resolutions.

For my part, I was ready to go home.

in hemingway's meadow

Jeff Day

The river, as Hemingway said, was still there. It was there in 1919, swirling against the log pilings of the railroad bridge in Seney, Michigan, while he fished it, feeding grasshoppers downstream with his fly rod and silk line. It was there in 1925, when he sat in a Paris café, writing "Big Two-Hearted River," the story of how Nick Adams found peace by fishing the river of his youth.

And it is still there in the summer of my fiftieth year as I unpack my rod and set up camp at the site where Hemingway camped, where Nick "came down a hillside, covered with stumps into a meadow. The river made no sound. It was too fast, and smooth. At the edge of the meadow, before he mounted to a piece of high ground to make camp, Nick looked down the river at the trout rising. It was a good place to camp."

By the map, the meadow is three-quarters of a mile long, and a quarter-mile wide. Behind me, at the southern edge, is the abandoned railroad grade that Hemingway followed out of Seney. Planted now with red pines, the old grade turns and then heads northeast along the eastern edge of the meadow. Along the western edge is the narrow band of the Fox River, the river Hemingway fished, and which took on the name of the nearby Two-Hearted River when he wrote his story. Lined by alder bushes and the occasional tree, the river slopes to the northeast, more or less parallel to the railroad grade. Two sandhill cranes—four feet tall with 80-inch wingspans—make their way through the meadow. They walk by giving their call, a half gobble, half shriek, as if I weren't there.

Hemingway told Gertrude Stein that in "Big Two-Hearted River," he was "trying to do the country like Cézanne and having a hell of a time, and sometimes getting it a little bit." He had summered in northern Michigan in the days when it was as remote as Alaska is now, learning to fish from his father, and spending countless hours in the woods with the local Indians. He wove what he knew into his stories and told them like an Impressionist, in scattered points of light. An evening dew. The water bucket hung from a tree. The way you pitch a tent. Coffee, brewed to the recipe of a long-lost friend and sipped from a tin cup. "Two-Hearted River" is a hundred stories in one, layer after layer, like a Cézanne painting. Underneath it all is what has to be the most literate camping manual in America.

You can see the pack as Hemingway describes it, the leather straps held together by copper rivets, the tump line around the head, the shape still molded to his back after he takes the pack off. The pack was a North-woods favorite for nearly a century, and was the first pack I ever used, a Duluth pack, patented in 1882. It is still made today, and the one I am carrying is packed with gear Hemingway describes: Tin pots I bought from an Ohio tinsmith. A silk fly line, made in France. Vintage catgut leaders I bought from a fishing guide. A bamboo fly rod, bought at auction. A blanket roll. A bucket made of canvas.

I will spend a week in the meadow, trying to see it the way Hemingway did. There was "nothing but the rails and burned-over country," he wrote. "The thirteen saloons that had lined the one street of Seney had left not a trace. The foundations of the Mansion House Hotel stuck up above the ground. It was all that was left of the town of Seney. Even the surface had been burned off the ground." Nick Adams, the sole character, begins a long, hard walk away from the devastation and towards the stream and the meadow where I am now camped. He has been there before and travels without a map. Trying to forget something he never names, Nick climbs a hill and then heads down to the stream, where the forest turns green and the water cool. There are two of everything, one good, the other bad—two ways to make coffee, two sides of the river, fish that inspire him, fish he kills. He loses the largest fish he has ever seen. He catches some smaller ones, and keeps two for dinner. Standing in the meadow, "he was there, in the good place." But he looks across the river at a swamp, where he sees life is hard, and the animals low and mean. He saves the swamp for another day.

Nick made camp slowly and carefully: The routine soothed him. I make camp carefully, too, but quickly, because I hear the river. Once my tent is up, I fill the bucket with water from the stream and hang it from a low branch. I step lightly on the grill to set the legs in the ground, and then put the pots on it. I spread blankets inside the tent, one folded in half as a cushion, the other folded on top as a sleeping bag. I button the tent, tie the pack to a rope, and haul it up 30 feet above the ground, where it is safe from bears. I look over the bank, fly rod in hand, and step in, still wearing my shirt, shoes, and pants.

In the days before waders and fishing vests, you waded in wool pants that helped keep you warm in the stream. You stuffed your gear in your shirt pocket, or, if you were a gentleman, in your sports coat. Judging from Hemingway's careful description of Nick's gear, and from early photographs, Hemingway was a shirt-pocket fisherman. He used an old flour sack as a creel and grasshoppers as bait, keeping them in a bottle tied around his neck. Like the pockets in Nick's shirt, and probably Hemingway's, my pockets hold an extra leader, soaking in a tin between damp felt pads to make it supple; some hooks, and lunch—hardtack, smoked ham and dried apricots.

My rod is bamboo, wrapped with red and green bands of silk thread that will hold it together should the hide glue that holds it together dissolve. It's a Hardy, worth maybe $200 or $300. I bought it at auction for $20. The silk line, one of about a thousand a year still made in France, cost far more. Nick paid $8 for the silk line he put on his bamboo rod— half a workman's weekly pay in 1919. Wages have gone up, but the ratio remains constant, and the line I have is a present from my wife. Each line takes four hours to weave, during which time the maker repeatedly stops the braiding machine to add another strand of silk in order to create a tapered line that will land gently on the water. It's a honey-straw color, and the finish that makes it slide through the guides on the rod has a rich, waxy smell. If I want to make sure it lasts a long time, like Nick's line did, I will not only dry it out every night, I'll make sure that it is good and dry when I store it for the winter. An old silk line I once bought was typical of lines that were stored wet: It looked and felt like new, but had lost all its strength. A slight tug snapped it in two.

But my line and leaders are good, perhaps better than the nylon that replaced them, and soon I am catching plenty of fish. The streams I usually fish are full of rainbows and browns, but these are brookies with deep red flanks, pure white-tipped fins, and backs of mottled green and brown. I stare at them and wonder: What was God thinking when he hid them in a stream?

Back at camp, I change into dry clothes and hang my fly line, which is waterlogged and beginning to lose buoyancy, in the tree next to them. In the morning, when the line is dry, I'll grease it, and it will ride high on the water again. In the meantime, I start a small cooking fire.

Nick's first meal in camp, and by default mine, was spaghetti and beans mixed with ketchup. The shiny tin pan turns soot black in the flames and I pour dinner into a pie-pan plate. The day has left me hungry, but the spaghetti and beans are a failure. Neither tin pans nor the giants of literature can save them. I promise never to eat them again, a promise that, by and large, I have kept.

There's a deep, red sky and Venus is rising in the west as I wash the dishes with hot water and a sliver of bar soap. There's no moon, and soon the Milky Way will be visible. If I am lucky, there will be northern lights, too, so I pull my blankets out of the tent and stretch out to watch the sky. Sleeping bags existed in Hemingway's day, but were widely hated, because they were heavy and not much warmer than blankets. "As to your bed," one old camping manual advises, "let us have one more whack at the sleeping bag—that accursed invention of a misguided soul. Leave your sleeping bag at home, or in the Minnesota woods or Adirondacks. Take a good pair of wool blankets."

I have taken a good pair of wool blankets (Nick took three), and in fact, they are more comfortable than a sleeping bag. Humanity has slept wrapped in some sort of blanket since the beginning, and the feel of wool, as opposed to the cold nylon of a sleeping bag, is comforting as I fall asleep. When I wake up, it is dark except for the stars. The Big Dipper has moved about a quarter of the way around the sky.

A great many things will wake me during my stay: A moose, snorting through camp; a bear, feasting on blueberries at the edge of the meadow; the howl of coyotes; and once the sound of a large, solitary trout, jumping and bellysmacking in the water. But what wakes me now, and what will wake me most often and most completely during my nights on the meadow is this: Since the beginning of time, no one, anywhere, has ever been as cold as I was in that meadow. The cold is deep and hard and slices through my body like a thin, metallic sheet of ice.

There are no northern lights.

Hemingway was 20 years old when the train pulled into Seney carrying him and two friends. "Seney was the toughest town in Michigan," Hemingway wrote in a draft of the story, and at one time it was: One street wide and one street long, it had 21 saloons. The three brothels in town competed with two more on the outskirts. With its wooden sidewalks and false storefronts, with the narrow troughs where the soil settled over the graves at Boot Hill, Seney looked and acted like a town from the Wild West. One bordello owner shot another to death; the survivor's father keeled over, dead in horror. The deceased's family murdered the survivor while the sheriff looked on. On calmer days, Snag Jaw Small bit the heads off snakes and frogs in return for drinks, and once taunted a barkeeper into feeding him by eating manure out of the streets. Old Lightheart lived in two sugar barrels turned end to end, ate raw liver, and lost his toes to frostbite. When drunk, Pump Handle Joe and Frying Pan Mag would nail his shoes to the floor, delighting in missing the absent toes. George Raymond looked on, reciting the *Odyssey* in Greek.

It was all about lumber. By 1929 the value of the lumber taken out of Michigan was twice that of all the gold taken out of California—and at the beginning of the Gold Rush, they were pulling $50,000 of gold daily out of Sutter's Mill alone. The first loggers to survey the area around Seney found pine trees five feet to eight feet in diameter. Needles from the trees built a carpet a foot deep on the forest floor.

The lumber that rebuilt Chicago after the Great Fire of 1871 came from Michigan's Upper Peninsula. Michigan lumber built structures in places as far away as Colorado, Wyoming and Europe. But by far the single largest log drive in Upper Peninsula history came in 1895, when a single company cut 185 million board feet of trees. Had the trees been loaded on a single train, it would have been 250 miles long. And then, like some bad cartoon joke, the trees that were eight feet in diameter were cut, shipped, milled—and turned into matchsticks.

The forest couldn't support the abuse. By 1900, the trees were gone, as were the 3,000 lumberjacks who spent winters drinking, fighting and logging around Seney. Across the Upper Peninsula, the slashings left by loggers were fodder for great fires that wiped out towns and burned the forest floor down to the sand beneath it.

It is on one of those sandy plains, a northern Serengeti, that I spend the night in my blankets. When morning comes I warm myself by the cook fire, and soon the camp smells of morning air, campfire, frying bacon and coffee. I sit on the bank, dangling my feet above the water, drinking my coffee, strong and black from grounds thrown directly in the pot and boiled.

The Fox is a small stream, 10 to 30 feet wide, dropping gradually, at an average of about five feet a mile. It is not a stream of *A River Runs Through It*, with rapids and waterfalls separating pools filled with fish the size of salmon. It is the stream of Nick's consciousness, barely a blue line on the map, a quiet stream, with a surface like moving glass.

Coffee gone, I step in again, flour sack over my shoulders, bottle around my neck. It is late August, the time of the year that Hemingway made his trip, a time when food is scarce in the stream. But the field is thick with hoppers that jump head high and blow into the stream or hit your face and fall stunned to the ground. I feed them downstream toward the moss-covered pilings that are all that is left of Hemingway's bridge and begin catching 8- and 10-inch brook trout. On a stream with a 7-inch limit, they are good-size fish. Any of them would fit nicely in my frying pan, but I let them go.

Below the bridge, the alder bushes have overgrown the stream completely and soon I am in a tunnel of alders. The air is damp and has the cold, moist smell of a trout stream, like the smell of a fall rain. The world has taken on the green of the alders. It is a close, comfortable stretch, perhaps 100 yards long and sheltered from the sun, an emerald world of its own, full of fish.

In the world outside the tunnel, I can hear a hunter training his dog in the high grass. He reaches the bank, somewhere so close that I can hear every step. I hear him talking quietly to his dog. I hear the dog panting. The bushes are so thick that neither of us can see the other, yet he doesn't seem surprised when I call up to him.

"What you doing down there?" he asks.

"Fishing."

"Nice stretch," he says. "Caught much?"

"Eight to ten inchers."

"Keep fishing," he says.

Did he think I could ever stop?

I work my way downstream toward the swamp that Nick avoided. The sun is high now, and washes the color out of sky and landscape. There is a second stretch of meadow to cross, and the grass is soon thick and over my head, a trackless jungle. At 50, I do not have Hemingway's teenage strength: the grass wears me out before I am a third of the way downstream. Unlike Nick, I am not afraid of the swamp; I am afraid I will never reach it. Resting, looking into the stream, I see an enormous trout.

"Jo heesus and be Guy Mawd Fever," Hemingway wrote a friend. "I lost one on the little Fox below an old dam that was the biggest trout I've ever seen. . . ." The trout at my feet shoots for cover, hiding somewhere in the heart of the river, and I know we will never meet again. Yet I cast relentlessly against the inevitable—lifting the arm and elbow, throwing the line back, reaching, as the man who taught me to cast said, reaching back briefly as if to scratch my ear, and then sweeping forward, pausing so the line forms a tight half circle that moves forward, unfolds and drops silently in the water.

The fish is gone. Making my way back upstream, I can almost see camp when I come upon a pool off to the side of the main current and shaded by a tamarack. The fly snags deep under the surface on my first cast.

But—another Hemingway dictum—the bottom never moves. It is a fish, and I play him against the springy tip of the rod, which absorbs the shock of sudden turns. It is not a heroic fight—he pulls more like a slow-moving train than a leaping prizefighter. I look at him before I drop him into the flour bag over my shoulder. He's a 12-inch brookie, and a week in the woods deserves at least one trout cooked over the fire.

Back at camp, I hear the call of the cranes, somewhere out of sight. I strip the line off the reel and hang it up to dry, next to the clothes I've already changed out of. I hear the stream, talking quietly, as it flows around the pilings. I clean the fish on a piece of birch bark, and use the bark to start a fire. It is a male, with flanks the color of the evening sky. The fire burns to coals as I pour cornmeal over him through my funneled hands. The smell of the fire, the butter, the fish, and the corn meal are more than excellent: They are the river's answer to spaghetti and beans, hard tack and blanket rolls.

Once Hemingway left Seney he never returned, except in his writing, which brought him back often. In 1920, as a reporter for the *Toronto Weekly Star*, he wrote of a nameless stream in the Upper Peninsula "about as wide as a river should be, and a little deeper than a river ought to be and to get the proper picture you want to imagine in rapid succession the following fade-ins: A high pine-covered bluff that rises steep up out of the shadows. A short sand slope down to the river and a quick elbow turn with a little flood wood jammed in the bend, and then a pool. A pool where the Moselle-colored water sweeps into a dark swirl." A pool where I drink my morning coffee.

"Big Two-Hearted River" was one of the first successful pieces Hemingway wrote. He was penniless when he wrote it, unknown, and discouraged. Everything he had written had just been stolen from a suitcase his wife was transporting manuscripts in. With it gone, he felt the need to start all over.

"What did I know best, that I had not written about and lost?" he wondered. "What did I know about truly and care for the most?

"There was no choice at all. I sat in the corner [of a Paris café] with the afternoon light coming in over my shoulder and wrote in the notebook. When I stopped writing, I did not want to leave the river where I could see the trout in the pool, its surface pushing and swelling smooth against the log driven piles of the bridge. The story was about coming back from the war, but there was no mention of war in it. But in the morning, the river would be there, and I must make it, and the country and all that would happen."

It may have been one of the last times he was truly happy. He wrote this poem, "Along with Youth," in Paris in 1923:

A porcupine skin,
Stiff with bad tanning,
It must have ended somewhere.
Stuffed horned owl
Pompous
Yellow eyed;
Chuck-wills-widow on a biassed twig
Sooted with dust.
Piles of old magazines,

Drawers of boy's letters
And the line of love
They must have ended somewhere.
Yesterday's Tribune is gone
Along with youth
And the canoe that went to pieces on the beach
The year of the big storm
When the hotel burned down
At Seney, Michigan.

frenchman's revisited

Robert Traver

It was a long hike from where I left my bush car into Old Frenchman's Pond, which I hadn't seen or fished in many years. On the walk in I kept thinking I was seeing deer, but they kept slipping away into the tangle of conifers like ghostly wraiths. My long march also seemed accompanied by the drumming of unseen partridge, with each bird winding up sounding like Gene Krupa on a binge.

It was late afternoon on a warm summer day and I was a carefree fisherman on vacation. When I finally reached the ridge overlooking the pond's old beaver dam and stood staring down, I wasn't quite sure whether the misty vision I saw was caused by the tears of nostalgia or the sweat of one pooped fisherman. Or possibly both. After all, fishermen on vacation are an unpredictable lot.

At least I saw no rival fishermen, so I rigged up my rod and took the steep, rocky trail to the pond and splashed my way along the old deer trail leading down to the edge of the dam. There I stood for a long time, watching the primitive fairy scene and listening to the watery music of the dam's overflow.

Looking around I was relieved when I spotted one of those rarities among modern collectibles; a totally non-plastic, all-wooden beer crate, upon which, after testing, I gratefully sat, waiting for the first trout to rise (or, with luck, possibly even a consenting mermaid with whom I might pass the time of day).

I'd reveal the name of the brewer I found on this crate, but I hate to inject even a hint of commercialism into the sacred rites of fishing. And, anyway, the cagey rascal has yet to make either me or my agent a decent offer.

My beery reveries were suddenly disturbed by the splash of a rising trout. It rose again, stirring me into action, and, still sitting, I worked out line and went into a sort of languid double haul and then into an easy, sort of dreamy, roll cast and presto, found myself onto, quickly landed, held up for a momentary ritual of admiration, and then gently released into the water below me, a genuine, honest-to-God speckled native brook trout.

"Real nice trout," I heard a voice say. "Seemed almost as long as a loaf of Italian bread," the voice continued, "Wups, I mean a homemade loaf of Italian bread. And I'm especially charmed to witness your release of that trout, a rare and genuinely gratifying sight to behold by the owner of the waters you happen to be invading."

I wheeled around on my trusty beer crate but saw no one. Then I glanced upstream and saw an old fisherman, white locks and all, sitting in an anchored wooden boat, a canoe paddle and a rod tip protruding over the front end, calmly peering at me over his glasses.

"Hi," I said, feeling myself flushing not only to be caught trespassing on private trout waters but to be caught in the very act by the venerable proprietor himself. "Didn't hear you coming."

"Sneaking up on trespassers is an art that comes with the years," the old boy said with a wry grin. "I'm an old hand at it." He pondered a moment. "But there's one thing that still bothers me."

"Yes?" I said.

"Seeing any trespasser ever return any trout, big or little, is such a rare sight," he went on, "that I wish you'd tell me, if you can, why in hell you'd hike all the way in here on a warm summer day and catch and then calmly throw back the lone trout you seem to have caught." He shook his head. "Seems contrary to all the ancient traditions of trespassing."

Though I'd never actually met the owner, I saw he was every bit the talkative tease I'd heard he might be. I also saw that probably the only way to carry on was to level with him. As that well-known philosopher Hans what's-his-name once said, "Show me a funny man and I'll show you a rabid anti-bull-shedder."

"I'm here because I love this old place," I heard myself saying as I reeled in my line. "Because I first fished here back when I was a boy. Because it was here that I was converted from using deadly live bait to the life-giving fly. Because all this happened long before you ever bought the place and barred it to the fishing peasantry."

"My, my," I heard the old boy murmur.

"Because I'm hopelessly in love with the vanishing brook trout," I ran on, "surely one of the loveliest creatures in all of nature. Because this ancient beaver dam, with its spring-fed, winding backwaters still lined with all those tall guardian spruces and tamaracks and all the rest, is one of the few places left in the Upper Peninsula of Michigan, or God knows, maybe anywhere, where they might still have a fighting chance to survive the planetary-wide depredations of our own species, sir—and I mean yours and mine."

"Hear, hear." I heard the old man saying.

I paused like a congressman in full oratorical flight and longed to be able to reach for a folded white linen handkerchief in my lapel pocket with which to delicately tamp my brow. But since pregnant fly vests traditionally lack the room for such niceties, I rose from my beer crate and pressed on.

"Because," I ran on, "I keep hearing reports that you've been sick, and lately I've been having night sweats worrying that the pirates among our fishing brethren might be raiding and ruining the old place."

"Pirates?"

"While for years I liked to think there must be a little good in every fisherman, I've now matured enough to know that some of us can be utter greedy bastards."

"Did I hear you say 'bastriches?'" the old boy inquired with a little smile.

"No," I said, "but I like the sound of it. What does it mean?"

The old boy pondered a moment before enlightening me.

"A bastriche," he said, "is the product of the very latest genetic tinkering and is a cross between the flightless ostrich and the slow-flying African bustard." He paused. "Some choosy dictionaries are still hesitant about accepting it."

"Oh," I said, holding out both hands, palms up, like an orating congressman run out of time. "Anyway, what I'm trying to tell you, sir, is that today I simply had a powerful itch to come out here and take a look."

I heard him murmur something but couldn't quite make it out. Then another trout made a splashy rise, this time over by the spillway, and about then I thought it time to leave.

"And after my brief period of invasionary research, sir," I said, retrieving my rod, "I'm happy to report that in my opinion the lovely old place has still survived."

"Well spoken, fellow fisherman," he said. "But before you start your trek back past all my 'No Trespass' signs and concrete-anchored cable gate, I'll tell you a few things about this place you may never have known."

"Shoot," I said, sneaking a look at the sinking sun and sitting myself back on the old beer crate and starting to take down my rod.

The old boy started to talk, occasionally pausing to squint down and pluck away at the stack of fly boxes he had laid out before him. Occasionally he chuckled as he inspected and found a fly that he put in another box. What he had to say was rambling and extensive, but if I am to keep this narrative under three volumes, I'll need to boil it down to about this:

Years before, when he'd first tried to buy the place, the then-owner had told him that he was sorry but that he was about to close a deal with a tree-hungry logger; but that with the timely administration of a series of euphoric shots of sour-mash bourbon he'd finally learned the amount of the logger's offer; that on that very same day he'd raced back to town and had a deed made, picked up some dough and then raced back with a kidnapped notary public, raised the ante and outbid the logger, and bought and paid for the place before the evening rise of the trout.

"And would you believe that the whole place—pond, dam, lovely trees and all the land around it," the old boy said at this point, "cost me less than the going rate for a pickup truck?"

"Hard to believe," I said.

"Small correction," the old boy went on. "I mean a second-hand pickup truck."

"Hard to believe," I repeated in an awed voice.

"And if I weren't so shy one might even say I saved the place," he said.

The old boy then went on in his rambling fashion to tell me how much he had hated to close off the place to his fellow fishermen; that in fact he'd left it open to all fishermen for several seasons following the purchase, in case I didn't know; and that he'd finally been forced to close off the place by—and would I please guess who—whom?

"Who—whom?" I dutifully came through.

"Our own bastriche fishermen."

"How come?"

So he rambled on, telling me that finally he'd had to hire a crew of experts and their equipment to come and comb and rid the pond and adjoining woods of the piles of cans and bottles and assorted rubbish our thoughtful brother bastriches had left in their wake.

I was silently shaking my head when several trout rose right in front of us, so once again I left my crate and made ready to leave.

"Aren't you going to give 'em a try?" I said, gesturing out at the watery rings the trout had left behind.

The old boy smiled and pointed at the dazzling array of fly boxes lying on the board before him. "Inventory day," he said. "Still working on the last box."

"You mean you haven't cast a fly at a trout all day?" I asked incredulously.

"That's right, young fella. When you reach my age you'll have accumulated so damn many flies and patterns you never use that you'll regularly have to go through all your boxes to weed out and retrieve the relatively few you do."

"My, my."

"In fact, I swear I still carry flies that Paul Stroud tied and sold me when he still worked at the old Chicago Abercrombie store when it was still called Von Lengerke & Antoine—in case there's still anybody around who can remember those names."

"They do sound vaguely familiar," I said.

"As well as flies tied and given to me by Art Flick, Frank Steel, Hal Lawin and others when they fished up here, though they never came up together. And by the old rod builder Paul Young, and later by his widow Martha, though Paul never made it to this pond. His favorite U.P. stream was the . . . but no, I'll not divulge it. Oh yes, and Morris Kushner, the innovative rod builder."

"You ought to be running for President, you'd have so many famous fishermen to endorse you," I said.

"No," the old fisherman said, shaking his head. "Primarily because of the risk of making it. And, anyway, most of the old timers I once knew are busy fishing off of Cloud Seventeen, wherever that is."

"I thought that fishermen never die," I said, ducking. "They merely fish so much they finally get to smell that way."

"I was still dabbling with spinning tackle when first heard that one," the old boy said, shaking his head.

"I gotta go," I said, studying the sinking sun and thinking of the long hike ahead of me.

"As for those reports you've heard about my being sick," the old boy said, "I'm afraid they've been overblown. That's unless advanced maturity and old age themselves are a form of illness. We're only young twice, as the old saying should but doesn't go."

"I'm puzzled you haven't cast a fly yet," I said. "I understand you have a mean, lovely roll cast and I'd love to watch it."

The old boy ignored the hint and went on. "Fishermen who cease sowing their wild oats and sow only rolled oats, and those only one at a time, become our genuine old fishermen. As the more poetic of the lawyers among us love to put it, I may be Exhibit A."

"Thanks for the visit," I said, starting to move away. "And I do hope we can meet and exchange some more engaging trout talk, unlimited, before another 30 years."

The old boy was back studying his fly box as I started leaving. "Come back whenever you can and feel like it," I heard him murmur. "Who knows, maybe I can still get in a few casts before darkness falls."

Once back up the hill I turned and watched the old fisherman still sitting there brooding over his many fly boxes in the dying sun. So I whipped out my tiny (and expensive) binoculars and beamed in and witnessed quite a scene. It seemed the old boy was actually about to fish and was busy selecting a fly. Two fingers were held poised above an open box as daintily as a lorgnetted dowager pondering her choice of jewelry for the day.

Then a good trout rose with a splash and the old boy closed one box and opened another and sat there nibbling his fingertips like a perplexed dilemma who'd lost his ticket in a Chinese quandary. Then the light began fading and I started feeling like a Peeping Tom watching a ritual I shouldn't, so I grabbed my gear and shouldered my faded packsack and all but ran back to my car, losing count of the ghostly deer that seemed to glide away to the ancient music of the whippoorwills.

Once out on the main road I was so pooped and hungry that I stopped at the first tourist haven I came to, wolfed down two Cornish pasties and then laughed when I found "Have a nice snooze," scrawled across my pillowcase when I hit the sack, signed, of all things, by the president of the motel chain.

Next morning I got up early, revived by the nice snooze I'd been promised, and was drawn back to the old pond as if by a magnet. After all, my vacation was nearly over and the old boy had invited me to come back anytime I felt like it, hadn't he?

I paused at the top of the ridge to see if the coast was clear. It wasn't, for there below me sat the old man in his rowboat, two fingers daintily poised over one of his fly boxes as in a kind of frozen ritual.

"Pick one!" I longed to shout but instead, on a sudden hunch, all but tiptoed down the hill and came up right beside him.

"Hello," I said, plunking myself down on the beer crate. "Sorry I'm back before my 30 years are up. Hope you don't mind too much."

"Welcome back," he said with a nodding smile. "Had a hunch you might show up. What's on your mind?"

I took a deep breath before taking the plunge. "I have an intuition," I said.

"Yes."

"I have an intuition," I repeated, "that all day yesterday, last evening and up to this very moment this morning you have not yet tied on and cast a fly at a trout. Am I right?"

The old boy peered at me over his glasses for quite a spell before he spoke. "Wrong," he said. "Fact is, I haven't cast a fly at a trout all this summer." He heaved a sigh. "Now you have my secret, Herr Doktor Kronkite."

"Care to talk about it?" I asked.

"Part of it may be repentance," the old boy said in a low voice, as much to himself as to me, I guessed.

"Repentance?" I gently prodded him.

"Repentance for all the trout I used to catch and keep and lug around the neighborhood and local taverns to impress the populace and massage my ego when I was young." He shook his head. "Back in those days trout seemed to run out of water taps, and we fishermen in our vast wisdom thought them to be as inexhaustible as the vanished buffalo."

"What's the real reason?"

The old boy looked over at me as though I'd just arrived. "Real reason?" he repeated in a low voice, then running on in the same low voice, not unlike a sinner in a confessional. "All fly fishermen are both slaves to and victims of their favorite fly. And hopeless misers of all their flies."

"Yes?" I said.

"So that by the time one gets as old as this fisherman he has accumulated so damn many flies, including favorites, that he finally lacks any knack of choice."

"There must be a way out," I said consolingly.

"He's . . . he's kind of like an oil-rich sultan who has finally gathered so many gals in his harem he loses the ability to pick."

"Powerful analogy," I said.

"Or the pep to do very much about it if he did."

"You might try barbless-hooked flies," I suggested.

"All of my flies have been barbless for many years," the old boy said. "It's getting so I hate even when I prick them."

It was then that the inspiration hit me and I reached into my tool kit —wups, I mean my fly vest—and found a lone fly in a little bottle and a handy pair of pliers and, presto, snipped off the entire hook and tossed it over to him. "Try this," I said.

The old boy gratefully tied it on and made a lovely roll cast almost across the dam. He raised a lunker, the trout fell back, the waves rolled out and the old boy almost wept.

"You've saved the day," he finally said, his voice cracking with emotion. "Now if you'll please lend me your pliers I'll get to work and repay you with my latest deathless epigram."

"What's that?" I said.

"Even the oldest of fishermen can live and learn," he said with a sigh.

author biographies

Rhett Ashley: "I am not a professional writer, but come from an Appalachian clan of story-tellers who'd rather tell tall tales than eat," Ashley says. "I live on the McKenzie River in Oregon, and have told such bold fishing tales (orcas herding salmon like cowboys herding cattle, which I've truly seen) that a fishing buddy calls me 'Mister Bluster.'"

Mallory Burton lives in British Columbia, where she fishes the coastal waters for steelhead and salmon and writes fiction.

Richard Chiappone is a writer and teacher who lives outside Anchorage, Alaska. He is the author of a story collection titled *Water of An Undetermined Depth*.

Kent Cowgill is a writer and teacher who lives in Minnesota. He is the author of *Raising Hackles on the Hattie's Fork*.

Jeff Day is a woodworker and home-improvement writer who lives with his family in Bucks County, Pennsylvania.

Peter Fong is a writer and editor who lives in central Vermont. "After years of publishing fiction in literary magazines, without pay, 'Letter from Yellowstone' was my first story to turn a profit. I bought a five-weight with the check," he says of his Traver Award finalist story.

Pete Fromm: Four-time winner of the Pacific Northwest Booksellers Award, Fromm is the author of *Blood Knot*, a collection of fishing stories that includes "Home Before Dark," as well as four other story collections and the memoir *Indian Creek Chronicles*, and most recently, the novels, *How All This Started* and *As Cool As I Am*. He lives with his family in Montana.

Harry Humes was born in the coal-mining town of Girardville, Pennsylvania. His poetry collections include *The Bottomland, Ridge Music, The Way Winter Works* and *Winter Weeds*. He lives in Pennsylvania, not far from a fine limestone stream.

Keith McCafferty lives in Bozeman, Montana, and writes often for *Field & Stream* and other magazines.

Bil Monan lives in Alexandria, Virginia, and works at the University of Maryland as the assistant director of landscape services.

Seth Norman is the book reviewer for *Fly Rod & Reel* and the author of *Meanderings of a Fly Fisherman* and other books. "Family tradition puts 1953 as the 'Year of the Coelacanth,' referring to both my appearance at birth and the subject of a *Life* Magazine photograph my parents pinned to my crib: 'As an infant you worshipped a primitive fish,' observed my father, 'which explains everything,'" he says. Norman lives in Washington state.

Joel Parkman: Raised on his father's farm outside of Clinton, Mississippi, Parkman often visited his maternal grandfather's farm in South Mississippi. In those settings he and his brothers learned how to catch fish with a fly rod. Later he was educated at Mississippi College, and did time in Texas, where he took a Ph.D. in New Testament Studies from Baylor University. Twice he worked in Moscow, managing an exchange program and working in the energy sector. Parkman is the author of the novel Earthing Man and a collection of short fiction and poetry, Poems and Stories.

E. Donnell Thomas, Jr. has published more than 800 short stories. He continues to write regularly about fly-fishing and other elements of the outdoor experience for numerous national publications. He has just completed his 17th outdoor book, an examination of sportsmen's contributions to wildlife conservation, due out from Globe-Pequot Press in late 2009. He and his wife Lori divide their time between homes in rural Montana and coastal Alaska.

Kate Small lives in Oregon and holds an MFA from the University of San Francisco. Her stories have appeared in *Madison Review*, *Boston Review* and *Best New American Voices*.

Robert Traver is the pen name of John D. Voelker. He was an associate justice of the Michigan Supreme Court when his novel *Anatomy of a Murder* brought him national acclaim in the 1950s and '60s. He died in 1991.

Scott Waldie lives in Montana and has worked as a fishing outfitter. His travel writing and fiction have appeared in most national fishing magazines.

Gary Whitehead is a writer who lives in the metro New York area.

Lyman Yee is a writer who lives in Portland, Oregon.